PRAISE FOR

DREAM LIKE M

South Asian Football Trailblazers

'Manisha Tailor has been one of *Show Racism the Red Card*'s leading education workers over several years, acting also as a mentor and role model to the young people she comes across in her work. I too continue to be inspired by Manisha and am delighted with this wonderful book which is full of many other people of South Asian descent whose stories also deserve to be heard'

Steve Goodsell, *Show Racism the Red Card*

'We enjoyed how culturally diverse the book is, like how the story remained interesting while also being educational. Manisha Tailor uses the influence of football in aspects of the different characters' lives, leaving a strong impression on the reader, making the book interesting and appealing to all ages and ethnicities'

The Reading Pioneers, Northampton International Academy

'Through the likes of Manisha and others sharing their experiences, they will inspire the next generation of South Asian girls and boys to participate in football, and hopefully help them better understand that there are increasing opportunities for involvement in the game they love both on and off the pitch. I am honoured to know Manisha'

Rachel Pavlou, FA Women's Development Manager – Diversity & Inclusion

DREAM LIKE ME
South Asian Football Trailblazers

Manisha Tailor

HopeRoad Publishing PO Box 55544
Exhibition Road London SW7 2DB
www.hoperoadpublishing.com @hoperoadpublish

First published in Great Britain by HopeRoad 2022

A CIP catalogue record for this book is available from the British Library

Print ISBN: 978-1-913109-99-8
E-book ISBN: 978-1-913109-04-2

Printed and bound by Clays Ltd Elcograf S.p.A

This book tells the tales of those who work in a variety of roles within the world of football, featuring those who are from different cultures and faiths within the British South Asian community. It highlights the challenges that they have faced and the strategies that they have used to overcome setbacks.

Throughout, there is an emphasis on signature strengths that have helped those featured to be the best possible version of themselves. *Signature strengths* are the positive components of your personality that impact how you think, feel and behave, and these strengths are considered to be a foundation for good emotional health, well-being and resilience in life.

The collection is designed to develop the critical thinking skills of children and teenagers. Specific questions to think about are provided for each person featured, to help readers develop comprehension, construct meaning and retrieve information. Alongside this, each account also offers a lesson to support good mental health – a lesson that young people can apply not only to their sporting ambitions but also to their everyday lives.

The following key themes are addressed: respect, hard work, inclusion, non-discrimination, resilience, growth mindset and goal setting.

Reading about someone else's life can empower the reader to respond to powerful ideas and emotions, and any connection with the experiences described is a valuable aid to help build the capacity throughout life to manage both adversity *and* success.

Manisha Tailor

To all those with a football dream.
To my mentors for helping me fulfil my dreams.

INTRODUCTION

Football. It's more than just a 90-minute game, or a piece of skill or coaching or officiating – it's a story. A story that reflects desire, grit and determination. A story that brings hope and enjoyment to many, including you.

I grew up playing street football in Germany and England and didn't join a club football team until the age of 16 as there was a lack of opportunity. However, I didn't let that stop me from making sure football would always be part of my life and, even today, if I have to break barriers to do so then I will.

And then the opportunity came. At the age of 18 I was given a scholarship to play in America while getting my degree. And that's when I really discovered myself. Who knew I would have been able to balance education, 6 a.m. fitness sessions, afternoon training sessions and weekly games (sometimes even two games per week) for four years? I believe that attitude defines the process. And football helped me build a resilient character.

Did I expect to travel the world with football, gain a scholarship in America or be given the opportunity to get my master's degree on a football scholarship? No. But I always dreamed big.

Now I am moving on to my new journey with freestyle football. Which is different to football but similar in many ways. Freestyle is creativity and unique to everyone, but still requires that resilient character and commitment to get better every day. Where will it take me? I don't know, but I know I can control how I use freestyle to serve and help others and I can control my work ethic.

This is just my story on football. Now Manisha has put together this collection to help you learn about others' experiences too. Hopefully these accounts will inspire you to create your own story.

Kaljit Atwal, freestyle footballer, UK

Note: The following chapters are organised alphabetically by each person's first name.

ABDUL HABIB

Using determination to overcome setbacks

For Abdul Habib, his friend's phone call was a game-changer.

'Abs,' said Anwar Uddin, the former Assistant Manager of Aldershot Town. 'Do you fancy doing a bit of scouting for us? Watch a few players and tell us what you think?'

Abs couldn't believe it. After years of toiling away in local football, becoming a scout for National League side Aldershot Town was a dream job that would add an important string to his bow. There was no money in it at the moment. He'd just be a volunteer. But that didn't matter. He was climbing the football ladder, and the money could wait.

As a football coach of Bangladeshi descent, Abs was already a trailblazer. Growing up, he'd played football, rugby, and American football, and used that experience to lead social inclusion programmes, after-school clubs and elite development centres while still at university.

His first job in football was in Gravesend, Kent, at Punjab United FC, where he was Assistant First Team Coach, before becoming the Head Coach at Welling Town FC.

Since then, Abs, a dedicated coach, has taken on many different roles during his career and loves pushing players to be better, on and off the field. He thrives on working with players of all ages, but especially enjoys helping youngsters. Of course, few careers are plain sailing, and Abs has had his fair share of setbacks and challenges along the way in a sport in which he's very much a minority. But he hasn't let that discourage him. Instead, he's drawn something positive from every negative experience.

For example, taking on a scouting role at Aldershot without getting paid was obviously not ideal. But Abs took the long-term view, seeing it as an excellent opportunity to gain experience as a scout. Even as a volunteer, working as a scout would grow his network and build his reputation. People would notice him, especially as a Bangladeshi scout. So he committed to being the best that he could be, working hard and always displaying a positive attitude – which has led to him gaining a role at Premier League Club, as Academy Scout.

As a scout, Abs's job is to watch players in action and assess their talents. He gauges their speed, strength, aerial ability, skill level, and work ethic. And he doesn't just focus on their physical talents but also on their mental capabilities and character. He studies the players, assessing whether they have the right attitude, get on with their teammates, and listen to their coaches. Armed with all that information, Abs then has a decision to make. Does he recommend the player to the club coaching staff or not?

Scouts have to be dedicated themselves, as the job can be extremely demanding. If he hears of an up-and-coming player, Abs has to go and see him play. That can involve hours of travel to youth tournaments, lower league games, reserve team matches, and occasionally overseas. More often than not, the destinations are not glamorous.

It's a job in which Abdul's under a lot of pressure. Scouts don't sign players, but their recommendations matter. Developing a footballer costs any club time and money, so the coaches must be able to trust a scout's judgement.

Abs strongly believes that football needs to get more people from diverse cultures involved at all levels. As a scout himself, he likes to challenge stereotypes. He wants people from all backgrounds to have an equal chance to succeed in the game and not be judged by their family circumstances.

Abs is a great example of what patience and determination can achieve, and he's committed to helping others like him find a place in the game.

LESSONS FOR GOOD MENTAL HEALTH: 'Try to accept that failure is part of the process and it helps promote growth towards becoming successful. Rather than feeling helpless and doubting your ability, see it as an opportunity to improve your skills and become better.'

Questions to Think About:

1. Abdul says that when negative things happen, they can be valuable experiences. Can you think of a time something negative happened to you and how it helped you to learn?

2. As a scout, Abdul will have to look at a player's skills and see how they fit within a team. Can you make a list of some of your skills and how you use them?

3. Growing up, Abs played a range of sports that helped him to develop a range of skills. What sports do you enjoy and what skills have the sports taught you?

4. What do you think Abdul means when he says 'stereotypes'? What can you do to overcome stereotypes?

What are this person's signature strengths? How do you know? Provide evidence from the text.

How do you feel after reading the story of this person's life?

AKASH MODHWADIA

Cheering on his local team from the terraces

As a true football fan, you live every moment with your team. The players' pain is your pain. Their joy is your joy. A football club is a family where the team, the coaches, the backroom staff, and the supporters are united behind one goal – winning football matches.

Achieving success is a joint effort, in which the energy bounces from the pitch to the stands and the stands to the pitch as the game unfolds. That's why playing at home is an advantage. With the home crowd behind them, players feel energised. And the better they play, the more the fans boost that energy by cheering them on.

Speak to any top player, and they'll tell you that the fans always have a part to play in a team's fortunes. When the crowd is with you, it's like having an extra player on the pitch. When the fans are against you, it can be like running in quicksand.

As a young Indian boy growing up in Milton Keynes, Akash Modhwadia learned all about being a football fan by cheering on his local team, the MK

Dons. The club changed its name from Wimbledon FC in 2004 after moving to Buckinghamshire from south-west London.

One of the main reasons for the move was to attract bigger crowds. And after a temporary stay in a small hockey stadium, the club moved into the brand-new 30,000-seater Stadium MK in 2007.

It was there that Akash would watch the Dons battle away in the lower reaches of the English Football League. But although the highest level they ever got to was the Championship in the 2015–16 season, his love for the team was no less enthusiastic. The Dons were his hometown club, and he followed them through thick and thin.

For most fans, watching their favourite team is enough. But Akash dreamed of something more. So, in 2014, he set off for university in Leeds to study strength and conditioning as part of a Sports Science degree.

With a job at his beloved Dons in mind, Akash jumped at the chance of getting real-life experience. While still at college, he volunteered as a strength and conditioning coach at several football clubs, including Doncaster Rovers, who played in League One at the time alongside the MK Dons.

In the summer of 2018, he completed a master's degree in strength and conditioning and went looking for work. From a local boy cheering his team on from the terraces, Akash was now a sports professional with a lot to offer. All he needed was a chance. And in October of 2018, his efforts paid off when he secured a job as one the MK Dons' academy sports scientists.

As a football fan, he was now living the dream. Working at a club's academy is an incredibly important role. Your job is to help develop players for the future. The academy is where young players learn their trade while battling to earn a professional contract. Good habits are formed early, and they can make or break a career.

As a strength and conditioning coach at the MK Dons, Akash focused on improving the players' performances. He led warm-ups before training and youth matches. He helped the players with their speed work and created gym programmes to build the muscle and explosive power that a professional footballer needs to succeed.

Akash turned his hobby into a dream job with a mixture of ambition, hard work and dedication and now works with MK Dons' first team. There are no short cuts. But by being persistent, building relationships, and making sure you're ready, willing, and able when the right opportunity presents itself, you can make your dreams a reality.

A LESSON TO SUPPORT GOOD MENTAL HEALTH: 'Take some time out for yourself and do whatever you need to do to recharge your batteries. This can help you to manage stress.'

Questions to Think About:

1. Akash has been a football fan since he was a small boy. How do you think that influenced what he wanted to study at university?

2. A sports scientist has a lot of roles in helping players. Which one do you think is the most important for helping players succeed on the football pitch?

3. Akash volunteered before getting his first paid job. Do you think it's useful to volunteer? If so, why?

4. Akash recommends 'taking time out for yourself to recharge your batteries'. What do you think he means by this? What do you do to help you refocus?

What are this person's signature strengths? How do you know? Provide evidence from the text.

How do you feel after reading the story of this person's life?

ANWAR UDDIN, MBE

A young Bangladeshi boy from East London wanting to play football

Football can be more than just a game. Whether you're playing or watching, it can become a big part of your life that keeps you entertained, out of trouble, and gives you a sense of belonging.

Anwar Uddin was born and raised in the UK to a Bangladeshi father and an English mother. The family lived in a tough East London neighbourhood. Fortunately, their home was near a local park, where football kept Anwar away from the crime and violence going on around him.

Like many British-born kids of his age, Anwar truly fell in love with football during the 1990 World Cup. For England fans, this was one of the most magical World Cups ever! England made the semi-finals before losing to Germany on penalties. Paul Gascoigne's brilliant performances and tears captured the heart of the nation. And the BBC's World Cup theme song, 'Nessun Dorma', was a smash hit with the viewers. England went football crazy, and Anwar was hooked.

Of course, part of being a young football fan is the dream of playing alongside your heroes. And Anwar was no different. Except that when it came to playing the game, he was actually very good at it. So good in fact that he was picked up by his local club, West Ham United.

The Hammers, as they're known, have a very successful academy system. And to join their youth team was a dream come true. However, it wasn't easy. Anwar's dad worked long hours, while his mum looked after the home and also Anwar's nan, who was severely disabled. Even getting to training was a challenge. But with determination, Anwar overcame the obstacles, helped by his sister and the club.

Being part of the Hammers' youth squad was a thrill. But training alongside some of the country's elite young players was also a little scary. And, to begin with, Anwar wasn't sure he belonged.

At the time, few English professional clubs had South Asian players. Bangladeshis like Anwar were known for playing cricket, but being a Bangladeshi footballer was considered unusual. Some people even doubted his ability because of his background. That put even more pressure on the youngster to prove himself.

Fortunately, Anwar and his dad had talked a lot about being the best Bangladeshi Muslim boy he could be and Anwar had been taught to take pride in his heritage. He also understood the importance of helping others understand his culture. He'd learned to use good manners, politeness, kindness, and hard work to make the best impression possible.

Anwar's strong personality caught the attention of the West Ham coaches. They saw he wasn't just a powerful and aggressive defender but also a born leader. And that led to him getting the incredible honour of captaining the Hammers' team that won the FA Youth Cup in 1999.

As skipper, Anwar took great pride in the job. Since childhood, he'd been keen on reading and learning how to improve himself. He feels the key is discovering your super strength – the thing you're really good at, or can become good at by putting in the effort.

At West Ham, Anwar accepted that he was not the most skilful player. But he was determined and had a knack for encouraging and supporting those around him. His super strength lay in leading by example and motivating others.

Unfortunately, Anwar never made it to the first team at West Ham. But he did go on to play for a string of league clubs, including Dagenham & Redbridge, where he became the first British Asian to captain a football club in any of England's top four divisions – an incredible achievement.

After retiring from playing, as well as being an advocate for equality and diversity, Anwar went into football management and is now once again putting his super strength to good use. In 2022, he was awarded an MBE for services to football.

A LESSON TO SUPPORT GOOD MENTAL HEALTH: 'Find your strength and think about how you can make that into a super strength so that you can be the best that you can be.'

Questions to Think About:

1. Anwar grew up in a tough neighbourhood. How do you think playing football helped him focus? Do you think football changed his mindset about his ability to succeed?

2. What characteristics or habits would Anwar have needed to have to be a good player?

3. Anwar's dad taught him to be kind and polite, as well as proud of his heritage. How would you describe your heritage and identity?

4. Can you identify your super strengths and how you can use these to help you in life?

What are this person's signature strengths? How do you know? Provide evidence from the text.

How do you feel after reading the story of this person's life?

AZEEM AMIR

Finding a positive outcome from every negative experience

Football is the people's game, which means it doesn't matter how old you are, what size you are, or how good you are, there's a form of football for everyone! And that includes those with some form of disability.

Azeem Amir is a British-Pakistani from Rochdale near Manchester, England. He was born legally blind, with no vision in his right eye and just a glimmer of light sensitivity in his left. But that didn't stop him from falling in love with football.

Of course, for Azeem, the sound of the game was the only way to experience it. And tuning in to matches on radio in the afternoons and *Match of the Day* broadcasts on Saturday nights became his passion.

Growing up, he longed to play the game himself. However, he felt that in the South Asian community, many people still thought taking part in normal activities with a disability wasn't possible. But Azeem regarded that as old-fashioned thinking. He wanted to prove to everyone that his visual impairment could not hold him back, and he became determined to live the best life he could.

At 15 while at high school, he was introduced to Blind Football, and his whole world changed.

Blind football is a five-a-side game played around the world. The strict rules require all outfield players to wear blindfolds so that the partially sighted have no advantage over the totally blind. The ball is filled with ball-bearings so that the players can hear where it is. A sighted coach stands behind each goal to help direct the players to where they need to be. Otherwise, the game is mostly silent, as spectators must remain quiet to allow the players to hear the ball clearly.

As Azeem's skills developed, so did his belief in the possibility of a career in Blind Football. However, he found the lack of training opportunities frustrating. If he had been a sighted player, he could easily have found somewhere to train at a local club any day of the week. But as a blind footballer, he had to travel up to 40 miles to train on a Saturday morning!

Despite the difficulties, Azeem's commitment never wavered. And with the support of his coaches and others around him, he began to make giant strides in his game and in his life. As well as studying Business at the University of Salford, he became the youngest-ever blind England international, making his debut as a midfielder for the Blind England National Football Team at the age of 20.

As a footballer, Azeem has weekly training sessions with a local coach, involving a mixture of ball skills, strength and conditioning, and recovery. With the England team, he trains at the National Football Centre at St. George's Park in Staffordshire, where the squad prepares to play tournaments all over the globe.

Azeem believes that positivity has played an enormous role in his life. He says simple things like an encouraging pat on the back have had a strong influence on his development.

He says the same teacher who advised him in high school also taught him that you can do anything if you put your heart and mind into it, whether in sport or education.

Azeem is also a firm believer in taking some time out to do what makes you happy for the sake of your mental health. He urges youngsters to be open about their feelings, to talk to people, and realise that it's OK to struggle at times. Through his success, Azeem is a great role model. He's passionate about the game and promotes disability awareness workshops to encourage a better understanding of people like himself.

A LESSON TO SUPPORT GOOD MENTAL HEALTH: 'Think of positive things that you can do when you are feeling low – it can be keeping positive by going for a walk, a bit of fresh air, food that you enjoy.'

Questions to Think About:

1. Can you name the ways in which Blind Football is adapted to allow the players to take part in the game?

2. Why do you think there were few training opportunities for Azeem to play blind? How did this influence his mindset?

3. What would you need to consider when communicating with someone who is blind, and why?

4. Azeem chose to put his heart and effort into football. What would you choose to put your heart and effort into? Why? How do you plan to achieve this?

5. Turn on the TV or radio and tune into your favourite sport. Close your eyes and think about what you can hear and feel. Write a description using imaginative words and adjectives.

What are this person's signature strengths? How do you know? Provide evidence from the text.

How do you feel after reading the story of this person's life?

BALJIT SINGH RIHAL

Travelling and connecting with different people

One of the most challenging jobs in football is that of an agent. They're the bridge between the players and the clubs. An agent's job is to get the best possible deals and opportunities for the players they represent. But they have to be fair and trustworthy.

The football authorities have rules to govern what an agent can do. But even so, some clubs are suspicious of agents. Many coaches and managers believe that agents deliberately encourage players to be dissatisfied and ask for transfers or outrageous sums of money. If the player gets paid, then so does the agent. And at the top level, some agents earn millions! So agents have to tread carefully, performing a tricky balancing act that keeps their players and the clubs happy.

Baljit Rihal is a football agent who specialises in working with Asian players. Baljit, who's from a Sikh family, grew up in West London. He was a keen footballer and Chelsea supporter, but a career in the professional game was never in his plans. Instead, he went to university and studied Economics and Information Technology.

But the football bug never really left him, and in 2009, he went to an event run by Chelsea, at which the Blues were looking for ways to attract more Asians to watch and play the game.

That meeting led Baljit and his business partner to create Inventive Sports in 2011. The company is involved in marketing sport, especially when it comes to getting Indian footballers and cricketers more attention around the world. In 2012, Inventive Sports arranged the first-ever Asian Football Awards.

The ceremony, held at the famous Wembley Stadium in London, was created to celebrate British Asians' contribution to the football industry.

It was during the awards that Baljit got chatting with a football agent. He asked lots of questions about the job and learned that becoming an agent is extremely tough. You have to study hard and very few pass the exam.

The news wasn't encouraging. But Baljit was up for the challenge. Asian football agents weren't common in the UK. But by passing the exams, he felt he could set an example, inspiring other Asians to follow in his footsteps.

The journey was a difficult one. But eventually Baljit officially became an agent. It was a big deal, achieved with hard work and determination, backed by the power of prayer and meditation, which Baljit feels helped him concentrate and stay calm when the going got tough.

As an agent, Baljit spends much of his time speaking with club officials and coaches to learn what type of talent they need. One of his proudest moments came early in his career when he introduced British Asian footballer Michael Chopra to the Indian Super League draft. The former Newcastle United and Cardiff City forward would become the first British footballer to play in the Indian Super League, turning out for Kerala Blasters in 2014.

That early success in India was hard-earned. When he first began visiting the country as an agent, Baljit was unknown. To get any deals done, he had to learn how the Indian football business works and gain the clubs' trust.

He believes that agents need excellent communication skills, as it's not always *what* you know but *who* you know that can open doors. To do a good job for your clients, he says you have to be comfortable talking to all kinds of people. Then, when the time comes, you must be able to work out a really great deal for everyone involved.

Baljit says travelling and making connections across the world are two things he likes most about being an agent. Football is his business, but it's also a very exciting way to earn a living.

A LESSON TO SUPPORT GOOD MENTAL HEALTH: 'Have integrity and be honest. Try to use the power of prayer and meditation to help you and others.'

Questions to Think About:

1. How did asking questions help Baljit learn about how to become a football agent? Why is asking questions important and do you use this tool to help you learn?

2. How do you think Baljit might have been feeling when he heard that very few people pass the exams to become a football agent? What do you do to help you prepare for an exam or test?

3. As an agent, communication skills are important – why do you think this skill is important in the role of an agent and in life?

4. Baljit was persistent and patient, which helped him to overcome challenges. Can you describe a time when you have been persistent and patient?

What are this person's signature strengths? How do you know? Provide evidence from the text.

How do you feel after reading the story of this person's life?

BELA SHAH

Breaking into broadcasting as a South Asian woman

Many people in football can remember precisely when they became hooked on the game. For Bela Shah, this moment came during the final of the 1994 World Cup, when Italy's Roberto Baggio shot high and wide with his penalty kick to hand Brazil the title.

The excitement of that tournament, and the penalty shoot-out's nail-biting drama, changed Bela from a casual viewer into a lifelong football fan. More importantly, it inspired her to dream of a football career, not as a player but as a broadcaster.

Of course, thousands share that same dream. And the path to success is challenging and highly competitive. But Bela was not discouraged. However, she did take a roundabout route, beginning her working life as an in-house contract lawyer at ITV Sport.

Her job with the network involved overseeing programme and talent agreements. Each day she'd study the contracts, and soon began to understand the wants and needs of the teams and players.

Getting up close and personal with those covering the game also allowed Bela to see what it takes to be a sports presenter and journalist. And it wasn't long before she began to believe that she could do it too.

Backed by her partner and family, Bela made a huge decision. She quit her legal job to chase her broadcasting dream.

She enrolled in an intensive nine-month post-graduate diploma in broadcast journalism. The course included basic newsroom training in editing and how to write and present a story.

When her training was finished, Bela began applying for every broadcasting job she could find while also freelancing to gain real-world experience.

Her first opportunity came in independent radio, where she read the news. She'd then go on to be a radio freelancer for the BBC, Talksport, and several local stations. But television was her true goal, and a job at Sky Sports News was her dream.

However, you only get one shot at making a good first impression, so Bela was content to bide her time and learn her trade before chasing the big prize. That meant that when the chance did finally arrive, she was ready!

After a meeting with the Head of Sky Sports News, Bela was invited to shadow some of the network's journalists and production staff to see what the job involved. Of course, she wanted to be in front of the camera, not behind the scenes. But sitting in the gallery was a learning process that helped her understand how a sports news show comes together.

Eventually, her patience and hard work paid off, when Bela was asked to present the channel's news bulletins. She made her debut on New Year's Eve 2018, and it was the start of something big!

From occasional bulletins, Bela rose quickly up the ladder. And in April 2019, she did her first shift as a presenter on the main Sky Sports News channel.

It was a proud moment for Bela and her whole family. Growing up in the UK, it was rare to see a South Asian woman in such a key role. She'd achieved her dream, and perhaps even better than that, Bela knew she was inspiring others.

Bela is now firmly established in the presenter's chair, working early mornings and even weekends on some of football's biggest stories.

Her advice to any Asian youngster hoping to succeed in a competitive career is never to compare yourself to anyone else. Just be you! Work hard, volunteer whenever you can and never be afraid of rejection, because every 'no' brings you another step closer to a 'yes'.

Bela doesn't regret her time working in law as it gave her valuable experience and helped build her football knowledge. Ultimately, it paved the way to a dream job that she loves – presenting sport to an audience of millions.

A LESSON TO SUPPORT GOOD MENTAL HEALTH: 'Remember that you are on your own journey. Try goal setting and focus on what you are going to do to achieve them.'

Questions to Think About:

1. Bela has the courage to present on live TV. What do you do to prepare yourself for presenting in front of an audience? This could be speaking in front of your class or whole school!

2. How do you think Bela's study of law and contracts helped her skills as a presenter? How could you use some of these skills?

3. Bela has to wake up early and work weekends. What habits do you think she has to keep herself prepared and on-schedule? What does your weekly schedule look like and what do you do to stick to it?

4. Bela says that you should celebrate your success. What are you proud of and why?

What are this person's signature strengths? How do you know? Provide evidence from the text.

How do you feel after reading the story of this person's life?

BHUPINDER SINGH GILL

Being inspired by his dad to become a referee

In football, the best officials are the ones who do the job so efficiently that you hardly notice them. But when the man in the middle is your dad, he's a lot harder to ignore!

Jarnail Singh became the English Football League's first Asian referee in August 2004. As a Sikh, it made him a hero to his whole community, especially to his sons Bhupinder and Sunny.

Like many kids, the boys wanted to be just like Dad. And Jarnail encouraged their interest in the game.

At charity tournaments for Asian teams, Bhupinder would run the line for his father, giving him his first taste of what match officiating involved.

In his early teens, he signed up for a refereeing course at his local county FA, where he learned the game's laws and how to handle being the one in charge.

After passing an exam, Bhupinder was soon refereeing youth games. But even at that level, the job was a lot more challenging than he'd imagined. As a young referee, controlling the players was one thing, but the abuse from parents and spectators was tough to handle.

After a couple of seasons, the stress was too much, and Bhupinder quit refereeing. Instead, he began playing football with his friends at Indian Gymkhana.

However, refereeing was in his blood. And when an injury ended Bhupinder's playing days in his mid-twenties, his dad suggested that he pick up the whistle again.

Though still unsure, Bhupinder realised he now had more life experience and man-management skills than previously, so he agreed to give refereeing another go. And it proved to be the right decision.

With more maturity came more confidence to make decisions on the pitch. There was also a lot more support for young referees than there had been during his early days in charge. Bhupinder had to be resilient and learn how to communicate and manage situations under pressure.

His experience as a player also helped him develop his knowledge. And, of course, having a dad as a top-class ref was a huge bonus when he needed advice. But Bhupinder still had to rise to the challenge. And he and his brother Sunny did just that. Both are now professional match officials in the EFL.

In 2021, Sunny and Bhupinder became the first South Asian brothers to be appointed on the same officiating team for an English Football League game. Bhupinder was the assistant referee and Sunny the fourth official for the Championship match held between Bristol City and Nottingham Forest.

For Bhupinder, many of his games are televised live on Sky Sports. That brings a whole new level of stress to the job, with his every decision in the spotlight.

To manage the pressure, he tries to ignore the cameras and focus on running the game. When prepping for a match, he shows up three hours before kick-off to relax and meet the other match officials.

After changing into their match gear, they then have a briefing about the game followed by a meeting with the team captains before kick-off to explain what they will and won't accept.

Bhupinder says being out in the middle means you have to be in the zone, concentrating fully on making the right calls according to the laws. The wishes of the players, coaches, fans, or TV pundits just can't get in the way. He also reminds himself that he's out there because he's earned the right and is good enough to referee at this level.

He admits that occasionally he makes a mistake in a game, which can be very costly to a player or a club. But in such a high-pressure situation, occasional errors are human nature. You just have to bounce back, he says, and remain confident that you'll do better next time.

Millions love football, and becoming a professional player is the ultimate dream of many. Clearly, most are not going to see their dreams come true. But Bhupinder says, you have to think outside the box, as there are many other ways to have a career in the game. He and his brother followed their dad and chose to referee. And I guess you could say it worked out rather well.

A LESSON TO SUPPORT GOOD MENTAL HEALTH: 'Mistakes are part of learning; don't be afraid of a setback – persevere and try again.'

Questions to Think About:

1. It is important to learn from your failures and treat them as opportunities to learn. Think of a time that you have had a setback – what did it teach you?

2. Bhupinder has to manage situations under pressure. List some strategies that you have used to help you manage stressful situations.

3. Bhupinder says that you should 'think outside of the box'. What does this mean? How can you think 'outside of the box'?

4. Who is your childhood hero? How have they inspired you?

What are this person's signature strengths? How do you know? Provide evidence from the text.

How do you feel after reading the story of this person's life?

BUTCH FAZAL

Not wanting anyone to feel like they cannot play or be part of the game

Football is the world's greatest unspoken language. The beautiful game brings people and communities together like nothing else. It's an instant form of communication that can make barriers like skin colour, race, nationality, and culture completely disappear.

As a young South Asian Muslim in the 1960s, Abdul 'Butch' Fazal fell in love with football. At the time, his family was living in a mainly white neighbourhood on the outskirts of London. There, Butch's father hoped his son would enjoy a more culturally diverse childhood. However, his mother was concerned that he wouldn't fit in. In the 1960s, people of colour were not as readily accepted in Britain as they are today. Even Asian kids born in the UK were often considered outsiders.

But Butch had a plan. At school, he began to use his love of football to get to know the other kids. He talked about football. He played football. He lived football. And in no time at all he was accepted as part of the crowd.

Soon, Butch joined a local team on which he was the only South Asian player. Unfortunately, as his career progressed, that made him a target for some people. For example, in one Cup final, he was told he was being left on the substitutes bench solely because he was Asian!

However, instead of fighting the prejudice he faced, Butch rose above it. By showing his skill and passion for the game and being a good friend and teammate, he proved that it doesn't matter what background you come from; you're still human.

Eventually, some of the same people who'd resented him began coming to his house, speaking to his parents and enjoying his mum's South Asian cooking. Many of those friendships are still going strong today.

Butch's love of football would eventually lead him into coaching, where he uses the memory of his own struggles to help guide and inspire others.

As the Coach Inclusion and Diversity Manager for the English Football Association, Butch works hard to keep the dreams of young coaches alive, ensuring that no one feels excluded from the game because of their skin colour. His focus is on Black, Asian and minority ethnic coaches, as well as female coaches in the professional game.

Butch's role is part teacher, part coach, and part advisor as he plans and delivers presentations and provides feedback to the coaches as they build their careers. Sometimes, of course, his advice may not be what people want to hear. Football is an emotional game, and it's easy to get upset if you feel you've missed out on an opportunity. But that's where relationships come in.

To succeed in his job, Butch believes it's vital to be a great listener. He says to work well with people, it's essential to build mutual respect and trust, especially when it comes to understanding people's needs. You have to be able to put yourself in their shoes.

Being adaptable is also important, as every person he connects with is unique and may need a different kind of approach. Butch feels good communication means giving straightforward instructions and advice. But he's also open to discussion, believing the best solutions leave everyone feeling happy and appreciated.

Like the friendships he made at school, Butch's successes are built on creating a bond between himself and the coaches he supervises. Only then can they open up, work hard, and become the best that they can be.

A LESSON TO SUPPORT GOOD MENTAL HEALTH: 'Try to find someone who you can talk to about how you are feeling and be honest with them. It is important to share your problems.'

Questions to Think About:

1. What does the word 'diversity' mean to you? Can you write down up to three examples of diversity, supported by an explanation?

2. Butch started playing football in the 1960s. Do you think the amount of diversity in football or sport has changed since then? If so, how?

3. Why is it important to be able to take feedback on board, even when it feels critical or negative?

4. How can you communicate with your friends, teachers and family effectively? What can you do to be a good listener and a good speaker?

What are this person's signature strengths? How do you know? Provide evidence from the text.

How do you feel after reading the story of this person's life?

DAL SINGH DARROCH

Making a difference to people and future generations,
regardless of who they are or where they come from

Everyone wants to make a difference, and as Head of Diversity and Inclusion Strategic Programmes for the English Football Association, Dal Darroch is impacting millions of lives.

Raised as a Sikh in England, Dal grew up football mad. His heroes were superstars like Paul Ince, Eric Cantona and Paolo Maldini. As a player, he was never likely to be in their league, but he did captain his school teams and played Sunday League football. It was the business world that beckoned, however, after Dal had finished college, and he began working as a management consultant.

Gradually, Dal rose up the corporate ladder, but by 2018, he felt in need of a break. Taking a year away from consulting, he got a temporary job with the English Football Association, working with the England Teams Division. These were exciting times for the England men's team, which made it all the way to the World Cup semi-finals that year. The country was buzzing, and Dal realised that the football industry was where he wanted to be.

Dal's background gave him a wealth of knowledge. As a businessman, he'd worked with many different people and cultures from all over the world. For an organisation like the FA, his experience with diversity was invaluable. He also had a background in youth football. So, armed with a range of transferable skills, he went to work on several FA programmes focused on people and culture within the sport.

He'd eventually end up as the FA's Head of Diversity and Inclusion Strategic Programmes. For Dal, every day is different and equally challenging. One day, he'll be looking at diversity programmes across elite England teams. The next, he might be discussing plans for grassroots football.

Dal loves the fact that his work will impact present and future generations from many different backgrounds. His goal is to make football accessible to everyone, creating a situation where people of all cultures can freely engage with the game.

But make no mistake, Dal's is a tough job, in which he deals with a wide range of personalities, from spectators to players to key staff members. Each has their own goals and interests, which Dal must take into account. But he loves the challenge and believes there's a road map to success.

First, he says, never give up. Plan your journey, and make sure you get the skills and training you need. He says it's OK to be ambitious, but success is about taking baby steps towards your goal. For example, if you want to be a coach, he suggests finding out what it takes and then plotting your route, making sure you have a plan B and maybe even a plan C just in case.

He says you shouldn't be too impatient to make your dreams come true. You first have to pay your dues. You can't be a surgeon without going to medical school, and likewise, you can't be a Premier League manager without first getting your coaching badges and gaining experience.

Dal is also a believer in taking time out to recharge mentally and physically. Sometimes you need a break to gain some perspective. His own short break changed his career.

Above all, forge your own path. Listen to advice but never let anybody make you question your self-worth. Achieving success is a marathon, not a sprint, so be sure to enjoy the journey.

A LESSON TO SUPPORT GOOD MENTAL HEALTH: 'Take feedback seriously and try to act upon it – never be too proud to accept developmental feedback as it could make all the difference in your life. It's about having a growth mindset.'

Questions to Think About:

1. Dal says 'you can't be a surgeon without going to medical school'. What does he mean by this?

2. Dal wants to make sure that everyone can engage in football. If you were Dal, what would you do to make football inclusive? Write down your goals and make it happen!

3. It is important to take time to recharge mentally and physically. Write down two ways you can recharge physically and two ways to recharge mentally.

4. Dal wants you to have a growth mindset. What does this mean? How can having a growth mindset help you to achieve your goals?

What are this person's signature strengths? How do you know? Provide evidence from the text.

How do you feel after reading the story of this person's life?

DAVINDER KAUR DHAND

Becoming the first South Asian female to own a football club

From behind the door of the conference room, Dee heard the rumble of chatter from the directors. They sounded lively and cheerful, like a classroom of children before the teacher arrives.

She smoothed down the front of her jacket and took a deep breath to calm her nerves. As chairperson of the football club, she was in charge. Though, as the only woman on the board, she often felt like an outsider.

'I can do this,' she whispered as she pushed open the door.

'Gentlemen,' she said, with a confident smile, taking her seat at the head of the table in a room full of men. Slowly but surely, the chatter died down.

Davinder Kaur Dhand, known as Dee, fell in love with football by watching the game on television with her children. But it was just a hobby. Then, in 2002, she got the chance to turn her hobby into a business.

The Middlesex Stadium, where Hillingdon Borough Football Club play their home games, was up for sale. The club was in desperate need of money and a leader to help keep it going.

As an Asian woman of East African descent, Dee was an unlikely investor in the team. An investor is someone who puts money into a project or business with the view of gaining an advantage such as making a profit. Few women hold positions of power in English football. But Dee was up for the challenge and bought the stadium!

From experience, Dee knew that running a business takes intelligence, know-how and hard work. Hillingdon Borough FC was not in good shape. Even small football clubs need to be managed properly, which means taking care of the day-to-day activities and planning for the future. The club needed someone to be in control.

Dee stepped up. She made sure the boardroom was looked after, the pitches were ready, the expenses and match officials were paid, the first-team manager had the support he needed. She also helped out with fundraising events and sponsorships to make sure the club had enough money, as taking care of business off the field can help build success on it.

However, despite all her efforts, Dee faced an uphill battle to be taken seriously by the directors. Though she did all she could to help the team, she often felt treated unfairly and not listened to. As a woman, there were times when her experience and business knowledge were questioned. She just didn't feel accepted, which made her frustrated and sad.

But Dee wouldn't quit. Instead, she used all her talents to win over those who doubted her. And talking to friends about her problems and feelings also helped her to find happy solutions.

As a chairperson, she had to understand business management, finances and how to negotiate and plan. She had to know how to talk to all kinds of people, adapt to different situations and work under pressure. In short, to be accepted, she had to prove herself. And she did.

Respect was hard-earned, but eventually she won the battle.

Dee would love to see more females working in football, especially in club management. Gaining respect and acceptance is still not easy for women in the game, but attitudes are changing. Dee's example shows how important it is for young people to be determined and persistent.

A LESSON TO SUPPORT GOOD MENTAL HEALTH: 'It is important to be persistent and not to give up. You have to keep trying.'

Questions to Think About:

1. Dee has one job with many responsibilities. What are some ways to manage multiple responsibilities?

2. What have you learned about the job of a chairperson? Can you find out about another chairperson in football of South Asian heritage?

3. A part of communication is also body language. When you are being spoken to, what kind of body language shows you are listening? How can your body language impact on how others perceive you?

4. Difficult situations arise for all of us. Dee believes talking about your problems and finding solutions with friends will make you feel better. Who do you talk to when you are going through a challenge?

What are this person's signature strengths? How do you know? Provide evidence from the text.

How do you feel after reading the story of this person's life?

DHARMESH SHETH

Turning the pipe dream of watching football for a living into reality

Sports reporting seems glamorous and exciting, and it can be. It's a great job. But because of that, it's an extremely competitive profession, and getting involved can be a long, hard road.

Someone who made the breakthrough is Dharmesh Sheth, who works as a presenter and reporter at Sky Sports.

Dharmesh was born in Tanzania. He's of Indian heritage and moved to the UK at the age of two. As he grew up, he always wanted to be a sports reporter, and football was his thing. As a youngster, he'd pore over football reports in newspapers and magazines, dreaming that one day he'd be writing them.

He even took a few sports journalism courses. However, there were very few Asian people in the English sports media at the time, and he wasn't convinced he could make it. So, just in case, he took a degree in economics.

But the dream was still alive. And after finishing his bachelor's degree, he took a master's degree in media communications. It was then that he got a massive boost of confidence. A sports interview he'd written up for a journalist friend ended up as a feature in the *Wall Street Journal* – one of the proudest moments of his life.

As a student, Dharmesh also took some summer jobs. And while working on one of them, he met someone who put him in touch with a sports agency. Ambitious and unafraid to push himself forward, he asked if he could join the agency for some work experience.

Dharmesh was accepted and got a priceless opportunity to write some of the agency's football content.

His confidence was growing, and so was his ambition. Though he was nervous about being rejected, Dharmesh called up West Ham United's reserve team goalkeeper and asked for an interview. Now, most reserve team keepers don't get much attention, so when Dharmesh called him out of the blue, the keeper was delighted.

The interview went well, though Dharmesh still had to sell it to someone. But as the saying goes, 'he who dares wins'. And after offering the piece to a handful of magazines, one of them said yes! Dharmesh had his first magazine byline.

Dharmesh believes that luck and networking certainly play a part in becoming a sports journalist. But he also says you have to put in the effort and make things happen for yourself. By going the extra mile and reaching out to a range of sportspeople for interviews, he managed to get a foot in the door and built a strong portfolio that showed what he could do.

And that body of work would later lead Dharmesh into television. He began as an editorial assistant at ITV Sports.

At ITV, he'd stay late with the editor and reporters to watch and learn how shows are hosted and how reports are put together. He'd write scripts of his own to show he was up to the job.

Despite his efforts, it still took three years before Dharmesh finally became a sports reporter. But his persistence paid off. Today, he's one of the most recognised presenters and reporters on Sky Sports News, even hosting the network's world-famous transfer-deadline day coverage.

Dharmesh's success is an excellent example of the old saying 'never say never'. He had a dream to work in a highly competitive field and now he's reaping the reward.

A LESSON TO SUPPORT GOOD MENTAL HEALTH: 'Be prepared and organised. This will help you to be less overwhelmed in all aspects of your life.'

Questions to Think About:

1. Dharmesh never saw someone who looked like him reporting on TV as a child. Why do you think it is important to have a role model to look up to that you relate to?

2. How do you think Dharmesh's experiences writing articles helped him when he was speaking and presenting on TV?

3. What habits did Dharmesh have at work that helped him show his boss that he was ready for his dream job?

4. Dharmesh says that being organised is important for success. What ways do you stay organised and how does it help you reach your goals or accomplish tasks?

What are this person's signature strengths? How do you know? Provide evidence from the text.

How do you feel after reading the story of this person's life?

GOBINDER SINGH GILL

Helping players manage the mind muscle
to handle pressure better

The late, great Dutch footballer, Johan Cruyff, once said, 'You play football with your head, and your legs are there to help you.' Cruyff's famous quote applies to kids playing in the park and football superstars alike. You need to be physically fit, but your mental fitness is often what makes the difference.

Gobinder Singh Gill began playing football as a kid. He loved to compete and quickly became a keen amateur player. But eventually he decided that he was more of a coach than a player, so he hung up his boots and put on a tracksuit. He also studied sports psychology, and eventually became a sports lecturer.

Gobinder was fascinated by how an athlete's mind works during and after a game. He studied how they cope with success and failure, and how they deal with the pressure of performing at the highest levels.

Using that knowledge, he began working with female footballers, student-athletes, teams, and individuals to develop mindset coaching techniques. His dream job came when he was invited to work with Panjab FA – a national team representing the UK's Punjabi community. As a Sikh, coaching the national team to develop what he calls their 'mind muscle' is a hugely proud achievement.

To get inside a footballer's mindset, Gobinder researched many different sports stars, trying to appreciate the various pressures they face and how they cope. He'd also watch games, hoping to work out what the players might be thinking. Using that information, he'd develop a plan for supporting his own players on the training pitch and in the changing room.

Gobinder says one of the big challenges is getting players to open up about their struggles and emotions. It's natural for athletes to be guarded for fear of revealing a weakness. A large part of his job is detective work, learning a player's mindset so that he can help them improve their mental strength. However, he says those he works with must be prepared to play their part by being unafraid to try something different.

Gobinder believes that psychology plays a major role in an athlete's performance. And he's developed many ways to help players become mentally fit. He believes having goals helps athletes focus and stay motivated. Gobinder also encourages stress management with slow, deep breathing exercises that help athletes relax and control their emotions.

He also believes that positive self-talk during training or a game can promote a 'can do' attitude, claiming it distracts the mind from negative thoughts and builds self-confidence.

Music also has a role to play. Indeed, Gobinder encourages nervous athletes to listen to music whenever they feel stressed. Once again, he believes it's a distraction, as focusing on the sound instead of the pressure of performing promotes relaxation and reduces tension.

As with any skill, perfecting these mind games takes work, and Gobinder encourages his athletes to practise daily, mastering each exercise in turn until they're second nature.

Gobinder is devoted to his athletes and says that nobody ever achieves their goals without passion. He'll offer his help to anyone who needs it, and believes the mind is a muscle that demands just as much training as the body.

A LESSON TO SUPPORT GOOD MENTAL HEALTH: 'Your mental health is important and in order to develop well-being you should develop psychological practices that prevent symptoms in the first place. Therefore, regular practice of psychology is the key to happiness and positivity.'

Questions to Think About:

1. Gobinder recommends setting goals, positive self-talk, music, and deep breathing to help promote relaxation and focus. Have you tried any of these techniques? What do you do to help you relax and focus? Which of these techniques would you like to try? Explain your answer.

2. What does it mean to say the mind is a muscle? What could help to 'grow' your mind muscle?

3. Have you ever watched a famous player or read about them to learn about their strengths or weaknesses? Did it change your opinion about them? If so, how?

4. Positive self-talk is an excellent way to build confidence. Write three positive self-talk statements about yourself or your goals.

What are this person's signature strengths? How do you know? Provide evidence from the text.

How do you feel after reading the story of this person's life?

DR IMTIAZ AHMAD

Seeing and helping people get better

Whether you play for your school or park team or turn out as a professional, football is like a family business. From the players to the coaches to the ground staff to the person who washes the kit (even if that's your parent), playing football takes a team effort – on and off the field.

In the professional ranks, a vast number of people work behind the scenes.

And one of the most important jobs is that of keeping the players healthy.

Dr Ahmad, whose family came to Britain from Pakistan, can thank his parents and his work ethic for helping him get his dream job, which combines two of the interests he had growing up – football and medicine.

As a child, he was encouraged by his dad to follow sport. One of his favourite memories is watching the legendary Diego Maradona lead Argentina to victory in the 1986 World Cup. However, he never dreamed of following in Diego's footsteps. Instead, from an early age, he wanted to be a doctor.

Encouraged by his parents, Ahmad began working towards a career in medicine. At school, he focused on maths, chemistry, and biology, knowing they would help him in his ambitions. Though he was a good student and enjoyed learning, he also made time for sport and having fun, which he thinks was important.

Dr Ahmad believes that taking time away from your work to enjoy yourself with friends helps you become a more complete person. It also develops what are known as 'people skills'.

He uses the people skills he learned as a youngster in his day-to-day job. As part of his role at Queens Park Rangers FC, Dr Ahmad deals with many different types of people. As a doctor and team leader, he tries to get along with all of them, which is no easy task when you work in a big organisation.

He believes that being likeable, trustworthy, and helpful is just as important as being hardworking and knowledgeable. Behaving with honesty can help you build and maintain relationships, whether that's at home, at school, or at a sports club.

At QPR, Dr Ahmad not only looks after the players' general health but also advises them on how to make the most of their bodies and how to be mentally healthy. He says you can take care of your mind and body by keeping active, talking to your friends, and eating the right foods.

His goal is to help the players perform at their highest level. To get the best from the players, Dr Ahmad believes it's essential for him to be kind and caring. He says you only get to know what people need by listening carefully to what they say. His hope is that when he offers advice, he's considering what's right for the players as people, not just as footballers.

Professional football is a huge business, and Dr Ahmad says pleasing everyone can be a tough job. But through hard work, he believes he's created an atmosphere where the players and staff are comfortable, and everyone is committed to getting better.

Remember that you cannot please everyone. However, by being open to listening, you can learn more about how other people act, feel and behave.

A LESSON TO SUPPORT GOOD MENTAL HEALTH: 'Try to be kind and caring to yourself and others. This will make you feel good and help you to develop empathy.'

Questions to Think About:

1. Dr Ahmad described watching Diego Maradona as one of his favourite moments. Can you describe a favourite moment – either in football or in your life as a whole – and explain why this moment is special to you?

2. What does Dr Ahmad suggest helps you to be a complete person? What would you add and why?

3. As a doctor and team leader, being able to get along with different types of people is an important skill. Think of a time where you have fallen out with a friend. Describe how this made you feel. What did you do to repair the friendship?

4. Can you list five key characteristics of a good team leader and explain your choices?

What are this person's signature strengths? How do you know? Provide evidence from the text.

How do you feel after reading the story of this person's life?

JARNAIL SINGH

Working hard and relishing challenges

When you grow up in a football hotbed, it's no surprise when you develop a genuine love for the game. Born in Wolverhampton to a Sikh family, Jarnail Singh fell in love with football at his local club, Punjab Rovers, where he frequently volunteered as a linesman for the youth team.

In 1985, Jarnail was invited to take a referee's course at Birmingham County FA. He was already at university at the time, but the chance to learn more about football was too good to miss. Little did he know that taking the course was the first step to becoming a role model and football pioneer for the British Asian community.

After passing his refereeing exam, Jarnail joined the Wolverhampton Referees' Association and began officiating local matches. But that didn't pay the bills, and at 23 years old, Jarnail moved to London for work.

For a time, he put his football ambitions on hold. But his interest in the game didn't change, and eventually he found himself back on the pitch, whistle in hand, on most weekends.

Referees officiate games or competitions. Their job is to explain and enforce rules, assess penalties, signal the start and end of games, stop play for reviews as needed, and inspect sports equipment prior to the start of games to check that it is safe.

Jarnail became dedicated to getting fitter and improving his knowledge and skills as a referee. Gradually, his hard work paid off. Moving up the ranks, he began officiating in the Conference South. In 1999, he was appointed as a Football League assistant referee. Then, in August 2004, he made national headlines when he refereed the League Two match between Bristol Rovers and Bury, becoming the first Sikh to take charge of a game in the English Football League.

Jarnail had become a hero to the whole British Asian community. He'd go on to referee more than 150 games in the Football League, as well as a friendly international between China and the UAE. However, his path to success wasn't easy, demanding a lot of hard work and patience.

Jarnail was 43 when he became an official for the Football League, an appointment that came after several disappointments. But he stuck at it, relishing the challenge and the role of being an inspiration to others.

Jarnail believes refereeing is about positioning and fitness, ensuring you're in the right place at the right time to make a well-informed decision. You also need to be a good communicator and have the patience to deal with different types of people! With experience comes consistency and courage, as regardless of the situation, or pressure from the crowds, you must remain fair and act with integrity.

Jarnail is also a firm believer that you get out of life what you put in. So, if you work hard and make sacrifices to achieve your goals, you will be successful.

He says the key thing in life is to have passion for what you do, because then it doesn't feel like work. Passion breeds enthusiasm, and enthusiasm produces results.

Jarnail insists that young people involved in football need support from family or guardians to help them with things like travelling to games and training. He also says that family members and friends can provide much-needed encouragement and someone to talk to when challenges arise.

A LESSON TO SUPPORT GOOD MENTAL HEALTH: 'Seek support from your family and friends as positive encouragement will help you along your journey.'

Questions to Think About:

1. Jarnail had to sacrifice working full-time so that he could referee on the weekends. What does 'sacrifice' mean? What would you sacrifice to help you achieve your goals?

2. Why is it important to have a passion for what you do? What are you passionate about and why?

3. Who do you have to talk to when you are facing a challenge or need encouragement? Why is this important?

4. Jarnail became the first Sikh to referee in the English Football League. What impact do you think 'being first' had on the community and why is Jarnail considered a role model?

What are this person's signature strengths? How do you know? Provide evidence from the text.

How do you feel after reading the story of this person's life?

JASJIT SINGH JAGPAL

Using education to gain a dream job

Choosing a career can be tough. During his GCSE years, Jasjit Singh Jagpal's career ambitions changed with the wind, from football to the police force, to retail, to teaching, and more.

Talking with his family didn't make up his mind, but it certainly helped. 'We support you in whatever you wish to achieve,' his parents had said. 'But with one condition. Education must always be the priority over all else because nobody can ever take an education away from you.'

His parents' words hit home. Get an education, and the world is at your feet. Jasjit went on to take A-Levels in Business, ICT, and Physical Education. Sport had always been dear to his heart, and as he began to narrow down his career options, a conversation with his uncle focused his attention on football.

His uncle had recently completed his FA Level 1 Coaching Badge and was volunteering as a coach on weekends with a team in Leeds. As a first step on the football ladder, he suggested that Jasjit start his coaching badges. He even called up the County FA to find out how Jasjit could go about enrolling for the course.

Soon, Jasjit had begun taking his badges. He also enrolled in a sports management degree at the University of Sunderland.

With his degree in hand, Jasjit eventually found his way to Sunderland AFC, where he began working for the club's official charity, the Foundation of Light. Before long, he began coordinating the secondary education provisions delivered across Sunderland, South Tyneside, and Durham. Some of his role focuses on the Premier League Inspires programme, which supports the tutors and teachers who motivate young people to develop the personal skills and positive attitudes to succeed in life.

In addition to his management role, Jasjit also became the organisation's Equality, Diversity and Inclusion Lead, enhancing the Foundation's effort to promote equality and diversity. This means wanting to make sure that everyone feels included and able to make connections through football.

Jasjit loves his work and feels blessed to have had people around him who encouraged him to pursue his dreams and never give up. When he first started, it meant finding mentors who would let him observe and learn from their example. To gain experience, he also had to work his first year out of college unpaid. But it was all about furthering his education with some real-life work experience that would help him become competitive in the job market.

Jasjit believes young people must listen well and be flexible. You may have an idea of where you want to go, but you have to be open-minded. Take on a variety of tasks and activities because experience not only gives you a solid grounding but may open doors you'd never considered. There is whole new world of experiences waiting for you to explore, and Jasjit knows this first-hand, now also using his skills at the Professional Cricketers, Association.

He also believes you have to take the rough with the smooth. Not everything will be to your liking, and sometimes you may not see the point. But giving your best, even when you may not want to, builds character and develops your skills, which may well come in handy in the future.

A LESSON TO SUPPORT GOOD MENTAL HEALTH: 'Be open to ideas and have the flexibility to try different things. This may introduce you to new-found opportunities.'

Questions to Think About:

1. Jasjit had a very supportive family, but they made sure that he finished his education before trying to pursue his dream job. How did Jasjit's education help him pursue his dream job?

2. Jasjit took a work placement position where he was unpaid for a year. What stressors do you think are likely to arise if you are an adult working unpaid? What could you do to overcome them?

3. Jasjit says to do a variety of tasks and activities, even some you may not like. Why is it important to finish tasks that you don't like and what can this teach you?

4. Jasjit says that you should try to say, 'Yes!' How can saying 'yes' help you towards your goals? Do you have to say 'yes' to everything? Explain your answer.

What are this person's signature strengths? How do you know? Provide evidence from the text.

How do you feel after reading the story of this person's life?

JHAI DHILLON

Moving from footballer to Rice n Spice Meals

As a boy, Jhai Dhillon believed he knew exactly what he wanted. He wanted to be a professional footballer. Watching his dad play for a local team, Jhai couldn't wait to get out there on the pitch and compete – and he was good enough to win Chelsea's 'Search for an Asian Star' competition in 2009 at the age of 14.

The path to success is rarely smooth, and at 16, Jhai left the Chelsea youth system to join lower league Stevenage FC.

Though he wasn't with a Premier League club, Jhai's dream was still alive. At Stevenage, he'd captain the under-16 side, and soon after he was offered a scholarship. Then, after a loan spell at Hitchin Town, he signed his first professional contract with Stevenage at the age of 18.

Jhai had realised his dream. He was a professional footballer, and in 2014, his potential was recognised when he was a candidate for Young Footballer of the Year at the Asian Football Awards.

But despite his achievements, Jhai had some doubts. He'd set his sights on being one of the best, but that didn't look like happening. And though playing at any level of league football is a huge achievement, he began to feel dissatisfied.

To play professionally, you have to make sacrifices, and there are no guarantees of success. You need to be mentally committed. But somehow, Jhai had fallen out of love with the game, and he began to wonder whether he'd chosen the right path.

Inevitably, his doubts, along with a few injuries, took a toll on Jhai's performances. And when a new manager came in and left him on the sidelines, he realised his life was at a crossroads. If he couldn't be a top player, did he really want to play professional football at all? And if he wasn't a footballer, what could he do?

While wrestling with the problem, Jhai spoke to his brother, who was running a food preparation business while at university. So Jhai and his mum decided to start something similar in their home town of Hitchin. At Stevenage, Jhai would usually be done with training by 2 p.m. That left him with a lot of spare time, which he decided to use constructively.

Jhai's new business focused on preparing healthy meals. He felt everyone would eat more healthily if it was more convenient to do so and it would be able to help footballers live a healthy lifestyle. With that in mind, the Rice n Spice ready-made meal company was born.

Pretty soon, the family-run business, which his brother soon joined, became Jhai's passion. The joy of creating delicious, healthy meals filled a need that football didn't. This was something at which he could be the best.

In 2015, Jhai left Stevenage FC and moved into non-league football. Here, he could enjoy playing the game without the pressure that goes with being a full-time professional.

Meanwhile, Jhai's business moved from strength to strength. Rice n Spice now has a small staff, and supplies healthy, ready-made meals to a wide range of clients, including several top-flight professional footballers.

In creating a business, Jhai found what he needed – a recipe for happiness and fulfilment. He says that when you love what you do, it doesn't feel like work. Football was his dream career, but the reality was not quite what he'd imagined.

A LESSON TO SUPPORT GOOD MENTAL HEALTH: 'Keep a journal and note down what you do each day. This can help you look back and see how far you have come and the progress you have made.'

Questions to Think About:

1. Jhai realised he could not be among the world's best professional players and decided to find another focus. What helped him to make this courageous decision? What would you have done if you were in Jhai's shoes and why?

2. Is it important to have more than one hobby or passion in life? Why?

3. Why is it important to try new things? List three things that you would like to try and provide a reason.

4. Why is it important to eat healthy foods? How does your diet affect your physical and mental well-being?

What are this person's signature strengths? How do you know? Provide evidence from the text.

How do you feel after reading the story of this person's life?

LUCINDHA LHATHINI LAWSON

Feeling proud to represent England and Great Britain

Football is a noisy game – at whatever level you play, hearing what's going on around you is a big deal. But imagine for a moment that you're learning and playing the game in near or total silence. How much more challenging would that be?

Lucindha Lhathini Lawson knows what it's like to play football in a world without sound. She was born profoundly deaf. And, as if that wasn't enough, she was rejected by her family. In fact, she suffered mental abuse for much of her early childhood and spent many years in foster care.

But in the middle of all that misery, Lucindha found an escape.

At the age of nine, she fell in love with football. And, with her natural ability and fighting spirit, she was soon picked for her school team.

Deaf Football has been played in Britain since the 1870s. Players take part in 11-a-side matches or small-sided games, such as Futsal. The rules are the same as usual, though you must prove you're deaf or hard of hearing before playing in competitions.

Lucindha had found somewhere she belonged and something to believe in. Later, when a young deaf man introduced her to the coaches at Fulham Deaf Ladies Football Club, she jumped at the chance to train with the squad. Of course, there was no guarantee she'd succeed. And Lucindha had to dig deep to prove herself. But, with the help of private coaching, she soon rose to the top level, where she trained with deaf and hearing players. However, even there, the challenges continued.

Communicating with hearing players and coaches can be a problem when you don't know what they're saying. And it can be worse when your coaches or hearing teammates do not have any deaf awareness training.

But Lucindha refused to make excuses or give up. With help and encouragement from her trainer and mentor, she overcame the obstacles and gradually became more confident.

Her talent and willingness to learn eventually led her to the top of her sport. In 2013, she represented Great Britain at the Sofia Deaflympics, the world's most prestigious sporting event for the deaf and hearing-impaired. In 2019, she was a member of the England Deaf Football squad at the women's European Championship in Greece and the England Deaf Futsal squad at the World Championships in Switzerland.

She describes playing for England and Great Britain as some of her proudest moments.

While practising with the English Futsal squad at the famous St. George's Park Training Centre, where all the English national teams train, she enjoyed high-level coaching on a par with any in the game. She got tips on how to develop her skills and tactical awareness, and how to eat right to maximise her performance.

She was pleased to find that the deaf players were treated no differently from players who could hear. And that was important to her, as she believes that receiving equal treatment encourages deaf players to be the best that they can be.

As a successful footballer and a survivor of a tough childhood, Lucindha is hugely grateful to the game for helping her become a strong and confident woman. And she's doing her best to pay it forward. By sharing her experiences and acting as a role model, she hopes to inspire others to overcome their challenges.

A LESSON TO SUPPORT GOOD MENTAL HEALTH: 'Motivation is what gets you started and commitment is what keeps you going. That is what made me who I am today.'

Questions to Think About:

1. How do you think finding a love for football helped Lucindha manage the challenges that she faced as a child?

2. Being unable to hear, Lucindha required extra support to help her, and sometimes the support wasn't available. What did she do to overcome this so that she could still learn?

3. After reading Lucindha's story, what have you learned about her disability? Can you find out about deaf athletes and the strategies that they use to help them as players?

4. Lucindha is a role model. What characteristics make her a good role model?

What are this person's signature strengths? How do you know? Provide evidence from the text.

How do you feel after reading the story of this person's life?

MALVIND BENNING

Using maximum effort and desire to prove your worth

In football, fairy-tale endings are part of the game. Through the years, countless young players have been told they're too small, too tall, too slow, or just not quite good enough to become a professional, only to prove the doubters wrong by succeeding.

Malvind Benning, a British Sikh, was a kid like that. Born in West Bromwich, he was raised in an area where football is everything. Mal loved football and put his heart and soul into becoming the best player he could be. Unfortunately, what he got in return was rejection.

Time after time, all he heard was: 'No.' 'Not this time.' 'Good effort, but you're not quite there.' It was hugely frustrating, and, of course, there were a few tears. But Mal never gave up.

He truly believed he had what it took to make it as a professional footballer, and he wasn't the only one. His father also believed in him and pushed him all the way to realise his dream.

Rain, hail, or shine, his dad was there to encourage him, making sure that his son didn't let the criticism break him. Not being too pushy, he let his son take the lead. If Mal wanted it, so did his father, and he was right there to support him.

Finally, in 2012, Mal's relentless persistence was rewarded when he was offered his first professional contract at League One side Walsall FC. He'd achieved his goal.

But getting there was only the beginning of the journey. The real challenge was staying there. In his usual way, Mal knuckled down, determined to prove he was worth his spot. Life as a professional footballer is highly pressurised. There are very few places in the squad, and it's a daily battle to claim one.

But Mal was a born fighter and committed to giving his best at all times. And it began to pay off. In 2012, he made his first-team debut in a game against Scunthorpe United. Then, in 2014, he earned Walsall's Young Player of the Year award. He was delighted. The extra work had been worth it, and he was finally getting noticed.

Sadly, in 2015, Mal was released by Walsall, leaving him heartbroken and frustrated. However, it didn't take long for him to bounce back. Mansfield Town came calling, and he signed for The Stags.

At Mansfield, he worked even harder than he had on the way up at Walsall, putting everything he'd learned into practice. And he had some excellent games. Of course, like any footballer, he also made mistakes. But he was determined to learn from the bad times as well as the good. He'd found a home. Despite all the people who had said he couldn't make it, he was a professional footballer, and life was great.

Mal believes you should never give up on your dreams. He says that setbacks will happen, but you have to push through them. He was lucky enough to have the backing of his dad, and he thinks the support of your loved ones is vital. Then, once you get your chance, you have to grab it with both hands and work hard.

Unfortunately, as one of the few South Asian players in English professional football, Mal has experienced racism. Naturally, the abuse and unfair treatment made him angry. But with the help of his dad, he never let it discourage him. Instead, the disrespect made him stronger, more determined, and increased his passion.

Mal, who later moved on to Port Vale, would love to see more South Asian players in the game. His road was a tough one, but he hopes his experiences will serve as an example to young Asian players, proving that you can reach for the stars.

A LESSON TO SUPPORT GOOD MENTAL HEALTH: 'Talking to someone has really helped me, especially when I have felt a little down. Find someone to talk to, as it will help to release any negative feelings.'

Questions to Think About:

1. Mal had great support from his father – what did Mal's dad do to support him? Who do you have that supports your dreams?

2. When Mal was told 'no' over and over again, he began to feel defeated. What skills were important for Mal to use to help him keep pushing through?

3. Is it OK to fail? What can failure teach you?

4. Can you think of a time you had to try a certain skill, technique, or learn something over and over again to get it right? What was it? How did you feel once you mastered it?

What are this person's signature strengths? How do you know? Provide evidence from the text.

How do you feel after reading the story of this person's life?

MANISHA TAILOR, MBE

Blazing a trail for others

Football needs heroes, and there's never been a shortage of dreamers hoping to play the part.

Manisha Tailor was one of those wannabes – dreaming of becoming the next Rachel Yankey, a forerunner in English Women's Football.

At the age of eight, she developed a love for football, inspired by her twin brother, and her best friend Jenna. Manisha would spend hour after hour practising her skills. She even joined the school team. But she soon realised that as a female footballer of Indian heritage, her future in the game would be limited.

At the time, few women of any culture played football seriously, and many people in the South Asian community viewed the sport as a boys' game. This situation made Manisha sad. She wanted football as part of her life, but the prospect seemed hopeless. What was she to do?

Despite the lack of opportunities, Manisha's ambition never died. Then, several years later, as a teenager, something happened to change her thinking.

Her twin brother suffered a mental health breakdown after being bullied at school.

The breakdown meant her brother found it difficult to manage his feelings. He lost motivation to play football, didn't want to talk to anyone, and preferred to be on his own. He was depressed.

Her brother's suffering triggered something in Manisha's mind. She decided she wouldn't be bullied out of her dreams. She would forge a path on her own.

Manisha became a primary school teacher. She loved working with children. And that, combined with her passion for football, led her to become a football coach.

Working tirelessly as a volunteer with local community football programmes, she devoted herself to inspiring young players. They were great days with some wonderful memories. But it was only the first step on a journey that would lead to astounding success as a coach and mentor.

Starting as a volunteer, Manisha got a job as an academy coach at Queens Park Rangers Football Club in London. In 2021 she made history by becoming the first person of South Asian heritage to become Assistant Head of Coaching in the English professional game.

To be the first, you have to be bold, brave, and resilient. You have to set clear goals and be open to different ways of learning. Most of all, you have to be willing to work long and hard. Put all that together and there'll be no stopping you!

Manisha believes that every young player recruited by a professional club has a dream, just like she did. She sees it as her job to guide them on their journey. Her aim is to help those she coaches make the most of their potential. She tries to understand their needs and how they learn best, creating a positive environment where players could express themselves without fear of failure.

Manisha's story is an example of overcoming difficulties by being adaptable and resilient. When the going got tough, she got tougher. And she continued to rise to the challenge. Manisha was also open to learning from her mentor Chris Ramsey, who offered guidance and encouragement to help her become better.

She believes that everyone deserves an equal opportunity to shine. And whether that's in playing or coaching football, or in another area of life, Manisha is determined to inspire all young people to chase their dreams.

A LESSON TO SUPPORT GOOD MENTAL HEALTH: 'Challenges help you to grow as people; if you fail, please get up and try again.'

Questions to Think About:

1. Manisha did not see many girls playing football when she was growing up. How did this make her feel? Do you think this has changed?

2. Bullying can lead to depression and anxiety. What is depression and anxiety?

3. Manisha was incredibly sad when her brother developed a mental health condition. What might she have been going through in her mind and what do you think she did to develop a growth mindset?

4. Manisha became a mentor. What is the role of a mentor and how can a mentor help you to learn?

What are this person's signature strengths? How do you know? Provide evidence from the text.

How do you feel after reading the story of this person's life?

MANRAJ SUCHA

Inspiring coaches and developing Panjabi players

Role models are important in any area of life, and sport is no different. Manraj Sucha grew up in a family of role models. His dad competed in Greco-Roman wrestling, and his uncle was a football coach, so he saw first-hand what it takes to succeed as an athlete.

As a football fan, Manraj also studied some of the greats, like David Beckham, Ronaldo, Ronaldinho, Paul Scholes, and the famous Manchester United manager, Sir Alex Ferguson. To be the best, it pays to learn from the best, and Manraj watched his heroes at every opportunity.

Keen and dedicated, it was no surprise when Manraj became captain of his school team. He was a born leader who understood the tactical side of the game. Indeed, he enjoyed taking charge so much that he earned a couple of nicknames – 'Scholesy' after Paul Scholes, the midfield maestro at Manchester United, and 'Manex Ferguson' after the legendary Sir Alex.

As a player, Manraj led by example. And his talents would eventually earn him national team honours with Panjab FA. Panjab, also called Punjab, is a region that straddles India and Pakistan. Its national team represents the Panjabi community worldwide, though Panjab FA is not recognised as an independent football nation by FIFA.

Manraj was a good footballer, but his ambitions didn't stop at playing. As a lifelong student of the game, he had an eye for potential and an ability to motivate young players to be the best that they could be. So, armed with a master's degree in sports performance, he became Head of Performance Analysis at Northampton Town FC, which he combined with work as a primary school teacher.

From Northampton, he went on to a string of academy coaching roles at various clubs, which he combined with working for the Football Association and local schools. In 2015, he joined the coaching staff of Panjab FA, becoming the manager's right-hand man as a performance coach and head of analysis. In 2016, the team went to take part in the CONIFA World Football Cup, which is a tournament for teams not recognised by FIFA. The competition took place in the Abkhazia region of Eastern Europe, and representing his British Sikh heritage was an immensely proud moment for Manraj. Signing autographs and taking pictures with young fans was a humbling experience.

Now he had become a role model.

Though they didn't win the trophy, Panjab FA did themselves proud, losing on penalties in the final to the host team, Abkhazia, in front of 10,000 screaming fans.

Step by step, Manraj was building a reputation as a talented coach. And after helping Panjab FA to a fifth-place finish at the 2018 World Football Cup in London, he was invited to take over as the new national team manager.

Manraj jumped at the chance. As a player and coach, his mission had always been to develop, motivate and inspire others. And the opportunity to steer his fellow Panjabis to greater heights was a dream come true.

The manager's job is a huge responsibility, full of challenges. Life in the hot seat is never easy, but Manraj thrives under pressure. Through years of experience, he's learned to adapt to change and react positively in difficult situations.

To get to that point in football, and in life, he believes you have to be willing to work hard to gain experience, studying those who came before you. He says you need to be curious about all areas of your business. He's also a firm believer in networking, because you never know when you might need to give or receive a helping hand.

Above all, he says you need to make sure that you enjoy what you're doing, as following your passion is the best way to build confidence and find freedom.

A LESSON TO SUPPORT GOOD MENTAL HEALTH: 'You may experience stress at any point in your life. You should never be afraid to ask for help that can provide you with tools to manage stress.'

Questions to Think About:

1. Having a role model can help us stay motivated towards our goals. Think of one professional/celebrity role model and one role model who is part of your family or a friend. Write down how they help to motivate you.

2. Football isn't the only place where things constantly change. Can you think of a life-changing experience and how you managed in that situation?

3. Adaptability is key in helping you through a challenging situation. What can you do to be adaptable?

4. Manraj was a lifelong student of the game. Can you name some lifelong learning skills and explain how you use each of them?

What are this person's signature strengths? How do you know? Provide evidence from the text.

How do you feel after reading the story of this person's life?

MILLIE CHANDARANA

Pursuing a passion to be a top defensive midfielder

Millie Chandarana knew what she wanted from an early age. Born in Manchester to a British Asian family, football was part of life. Her dad was a Manchester United fan while her grandad supported Manchester City. And their friendly rivalry only fuelled Millie's interest in the game.

At every opportunity, Millie would be outside practising her football skills. In the house, she'd spend hours watching games. Her favourite player was the Brazilian legend, Ronaldinho, whose mesmerising skills and showmanship had Millie hooked.

At the age of eight, she tried out for the boys' team at her school. But it wasn't a fairy-tale beginning, as she scored an own goal from the halfway line! But Millie wasn't discouraged, and a few months later, she tried out for the boys' team again. This time she got in.

With the support of her family, Millie's football career was up and running. Two years later, she joined the Manchester United Centre of Excellence Academy, where she received expert coaching. And before too long, she found herself in the Women's Premier League playing for Blackburn Rovers. Millie was a hot prospect, a defensive midfielder with talent and dedication. She spent two years with Rovers, even making it to the FA Youth Cup Final against Arsenal. But football wasn't Millie's only goal. She wanted an education, and in 2015, she won a place at the famous Loughborough University to study Sport and Exercise Science.

While taking her degree, Millie played for the Loughborough University team, and after graduating, she joined Loughborough Foxes LFC in the third tier of English women's football. She then spent a year in Dubai, working as a health and wellness coach and playing football part-time for Leoni FC. But it was in July of 2019 that she got her biggest break when she signed as a full-time professional footballer with Italian Serie A side, UPC Tavagnacco.

The move to Italy was an honour and a challenge, and one that she is relishing. Millie was humbled by playing with girls of all nationalities, races, and religions. It was inspirational to see how football brought so many different people together. And as a British-Asian, she was proud to represent her culture.

On the field, Millie never stopped pushing herself. She was always eager to learn new things and was open to different opportunities. As a professional footballer, Millie would play once or twice a week and train at least five times per week. It was hard work, but Millie stayed focused.

A major highlight of her career was scoring her first goal for Tavagnacco, which came against the women of Italian giants, Juventus. That, she says, is something she will never forget.

Millie says being a footballer is a demanding job and can involve a lot of change. You might be at a club one season, and then another club the next – she has found herself moving from Tavagnacco to San Marino Academy to back to England, currently playing for Blackburn Rovers. You have to be confident, disciplined, persistent, and determined to succeed. Pursuing her career in Italy was a big risk, and she admits that the life-changing decision was pretty scary. But looking back, Millie says she wouldn't have changed a thing. Without risk, there can be no reward, and the chances she took made Millie's dream a reality.

Millie thinks football is a brilliant way to meet people, make social and business connections, and gain lifelong friends. By being true to yourself, pursuing your passion, and working hard, she believes you create your own opportunities to get what you want. You should never give up. Keep trying, keep exploring, keep challenging yourself until you find your path.

A LESSON TO SUPPORT GOOD MENTAL HEALTH: 'Don't worry or stress about the past or the future, because the most important time is now. If you work hard and enjoy what you do, everything will work out eventually. Stay in the moment and enjoy it. After that, enjoy the change that follows.'

Questions to Think About:

1. How do you think Millie felt as a young child when she kicked the ball into the wrong goal? What made Millie brave enough to keep pursuing football after that mistake?

2. What skills or habits do you think were important for Millie to have to be a good student and a good footballer?

3. Millie took some big risks. Think of a risk you would take to help you reach your goal. What would you do to help you work towards it?

4. Millie travelled all over the world. What skills or personality traits do you think she developed to help her meet and work with people from different backgrounds?

What are this person's signature strengths? How do you know? Provide evidence from the text.

How do you feel after reading the story of this person's life?

MONICA SHAFAQ

Ensuring women take a seat at the table

Monica Shafaq has spent her career focusing on emotional health and well-being. She is Chief Executive for The Kaleidoscope Plus Group, a national health and well-being organisation that focuses on mental health.

Monica believes surrounding herself with people with different skills and diverse experiences is vital to success in her profession, and she feels the same is true for football.

Football is a male-dominated industry and one in which people from different diverse backgrounds seem to be invisible at a senior level. As a woman of Indian heritage, this is something Monica aspires to change.

She believes that women need a seat at the table, and perhaps in some cases, a table of their own. Significant change, she says, must be led from the top, where a change in executive culture can result in decisions that make a real impact.

Since Monica's profession isn't in football, she needed to work extra hard to establish a network among sportspeople. She had to be actively involved in events, workshops, and discussion groups to become familiar with how the world of football operates. Her efforts had benefits for all, as others had to become familiar with her experiences and knowledge too.

Monica sits on the boards of Kidderminster Harriers FC and the Birmingham County FA, and is committed to having a positive long-term effect. Her role is to make strategic business decisions. These could relate to policy, jobs, or how to spend money, any of which could affect staff, fans, and players at all levels.

Her choices could also impact the wider community because football isn't just a sport. The game touches lives, and can influence many social and economic issues. Monica keeps that at the forefront of her mind whenever she has to make a decision.

Monica faces unique challenges in a world where a woman of colour is in a tiny minority. But the biggest challenge she faced was at the beginning, trying to get into the football industry at all!

She couldn't play the game and knew little about the laws or culture. But instead of feeling insecure, she demonstrated her value by showing how her knowledge, skills, and experience in other walks of life could be applied to football. Her transferable skillset.

Monica knows that creating equality and diversity in the workplace isn't just about employing people of different genders and backgrounds. It also means having individuals with a diverse set of skills that can help bring about positive change.

Life presents challenges, no matter what job you choose. To have good emotional well-being is to have a sense of purpose and an understanding and acceptance of who *you* are. Decide what you want in life. Even if you don't have the plan yet, you must have direction or a vision for your future.

Believe in yourself. There is no one else in the world like you. What you have to offer is something that no one else has. You are unique. Be the real you, and always remember that when challenges present themselves, remain determined.

As you grow, surround yourself with those who will help you in your aims, encourage, motivate, and cheer you on – those are your people.

A LESSON TO SUPPORT GOOD MENTAL HEALTH: 'Self-care and compassion are important. Take time out to look after yourself, whether that be simply having a soak in the bath, exercising, meeting friends, or anything else that helps you to switch off and relax.'

Questions to Think About:

1. What do you understand by 'transferable skillset'? Can you name a range of skills that you would use in one sport or subject that you would also use in life?

2. Monica wants you to surround yourself with the people who cheer you on and motivate you. Make a list of three of those people in your life and how they provide you with positive energy.

3. You are unique and original; no one in the history of the Earth has been born that is exactly like you. Write three things down you love about yourself – go back to this list when you feel a little low or sad.

4. Taking on a job or completing a project that you have no experience in can be intimidating. Write down three ways you can prepare for trying something new. Try to bring these into action and write about how it went.

What are this person's signature strengths? How do you know? Provide evidence from the text.

How do you feel after reading the story of this person's life?

MUKESH SINGH TALWAR

Being the best that you can be

Mukesh Singh Talwar can still recall how his interest in football began. His dad took Mukesh and his little brother to their first professional game when Mukesh was ten years old. Nottingham Forest against Walsall, some would say, isn't the most glamorous fixture in English football, but the noise and excitement of the fans and the skill of the players left a big impression on the youngster.

As a British-Indian, Mukesh had few role models to look up to in the English game. But football fascinated him. And from early on, he dreamed of making it a career.

However, short of becoming a player, which Mukesh knew was a bit of a long shot, how was he going to break into the sport?

At the time, there were few Asians in English football, on or off the pitch. But when Mukesh told his mum and grandad about his dream to work in the game, they were supportive and encouraging.

During his final year at the University of Worcester, Mukesh studied performance analysis. On the first day of classes, he learned there were several places where students could get work experience. One of them was Wolverhampton Wanderers Football Club. Mukesh jumped at the chance. And soon after, he began working for Wolves as a volunteer performance analyst.

Using technology and statistics to analyse footballers and football matches has not been around that long. As recently as 2005, many top managers saw it as overkill, something that they saw as being used too much. But in the modern game, performance analysis plays a crucial role in helping teams and players succeed.

In 2016, Mukesh left university with a bachelor's degree in Physical Education and Sports Coaching Science and some priceless experience with a professional football club. He was ready to take the next step.

However, jobs in his field were hard to come by. Mukesh continued his volunteer work with Wolves, and also Kidderminster Harriers FC, but it wasn't paying the bills.

He wondered how much longer he could keep his dream alive without earning any money. But, with his family's backing, he kept going, determined to get as much experience as possible to ensure he was ready if a job came up. Eventually his sacrifice paid off when he landed a full-time job as a performance analyst at Birmingham City Football Club. It's important work, involving overseeing pre- and post-match analysis and providing detailed evidence to players and coaches about their own performances. In addition, Mukesh has to compile statistics on the opposition and supply video clips of triallists hoping to sign for the club.

Now at Sheffield United, Mukesh says one of the things he most enjoys is seeing young players progress to the first team. As an analyst, he plays a part in their success, and he feels driven to help others achieve their goals.

Mukesh is a great example of being the best that you can be. However, he also stresses the importance of knowing when to switch off and relax. Spending time with family and friends can improve your mental health and help you have a fresh outlook on life, even when your life is as cool and rewarding as his.

A LESSON TO SUPPORT GOOD MENTAL HEALTH: 'Spending time with family and friends is good way of helping your mind recharge.'

Questions to Think About:

1. What helped Mukesh keep his dream of working in football alive? Do you think he would have achieved his dream job without this?

2. What is one tool you could use to help you manage your time to ensure you reach your goals without burning out?

3. How does spending time with family or friends help with your mental health? How did it help Mukesh?

4. Mukesh feels driven to help players achieve their dreams. Can you give an example of when you have helped someone else? How did this make you feel?

What are this person's signature strengths? How do you know? Provide evidence from the text.

How do you feel after reading the story of this person's life?

NAV SINGH

Applying scientific knowledge and techniques

Everyone needs role models, and Nav Singh was lucky enough to have a few. There were his brothers, who he loved to watch playing football, and the former Arsenal and France superstar, Thierry Henry.

As a youngster, Nav was fascinated by what made a world-class athlete. And his interest would eventually lead him to rub shoulders with many top athletes as a sports scientist at Arsenal Football Club.

Working with elite professional footballers from the first team to the academy, Nav's job is to help professional footballers achieve their best performance by applying scientific knowledge and techniques from sports sciences, such as physiology and biomechanics. It's demanding work in which Nav learns something new every day about the human body and how to create better footballers.

Though he was thrilled to be involved, Nav initially found the job at Arsenal pretty tough. To succeed and prove himself, he had to learn quickly, study hard, and change his mindset.

Sports science isn't a traditional role. When he started, there were no paid positions in football for his skills. That meant he had to take another job to earn a living while working as a club volunteer. He would travel three hours from his family home in Grimsby to Arsenal's training ground in London, then drive back for three hours. He did that for four years!

Despite the long commute, Nav believed it would lead to an opportunity. And eventually it did, when a chance arose to work with the first team. After a three-month trial, he was taken on full-time.

Nav was living the dream. He even played a part in helping Arsenal win the FA Cup, getting to lift the trophy alongside world-class players, staff, and manager Arsene Wenger.

But it could all have been so different. Like most Indian families, Nav's had wanted him to use his education to get a steady job that made him financially secure. However, he had a dream and was determined to pursue it, even though he had no idea if he could succeed.

Fortunately, Nav did succeed, but it was hard to share his ambitions and achievements with his family. They just didn't see football the same way as he did. That, he believes, is a life lesson.

During his football career, Nav has had to support himself mentally. The path he took has been lonely as there are not many people in English football from an Asian background. Without that understanding and support, Nav had to rely on people that couldn't relate to his culture. And, of course, that made things harder.

He put a lot of pressure on himself to impress others and show that he could work at the highest level. That meant going the extra mile and putting his career before anything else.

To anyone that wishes to work in football, Nav strongly advises the following:

Get an education. You must specialise in an area that separates you from the rest. You should learn all you can about the career you wish to follow.

Gain experience, even if it's unpaid. Nav's most triumphant moments came from volunteering and showing his drive to learn without monetary gain.

Find a mentor. Ensure you reach out to someone specialising in the field you are interested in and ask them to help guide you.

A LESSON TO SUPPORT GOOD MENTAL HEALTH: 'Self Respect – Establish YOUR personal values and beliefs and make sure you live them truly and reflect on them regularly as this will keep you anchored in life no matter the situation. Do not change them based on what others expect.'

Questions to Think About:

1. Initially, Nav's family didn't really understand his career choice. How do you think that helped or hurt his progress towards his goals?

2. Nav always went the extra mile to prove his worth. What impact do you think that could have on his mental health? Why?

3. Nav stated the importance of finding a mentor. What is a mentor? Who do you have as a mentor and how does this person help you?

4. What does self-respect mean to you? Can you create your own personal values charter that you live by on a daily basis?

What are this person's signature strengths? How do you know? Provide evidence from the text.

How do you feel after reading the story of this person's life?

NEIL TAYLOR

Embracing change to reach your goals

Neil Taylor was just a young child when his dreams of playing professional football began. Inspired by his older brother, he loved the game. But in the small town of Ruthin, North Wales, there weren't many options to play competitively. Fortunately, his parents decided to move the family closer to the English border, where there were more opportunities for him.

At the age of seven, he was good enough to earn a trial with Manchester City. And, despite his nerves, City liked what they saw, and invited him to join the club's youth system.

Neil would spend eight years at City's academy, where he was groomed for a top-flight career. The family's home was an hour and a half from the training ground, where Neil travelled three times a week to train or play matches.

Neil's parents were fully behind him, giving up their weekends to drive him around. They also helped him balance his sporting activities with his school work, ensuring that he never fell behind in the classroom or felt too much pressure to perform on the sports field.

With such a busy schedule, Neil made many sacrifices, but it was a price he was ready to pay to realise his dream of becoming a professional athlete.

His dedication was impressive, but football is a tough business in which only a very few make the grade. Unfortunately, at City, Neil was not one of them. Being told he wasn't good enough was a bitter pill to swallow. Not only was he heartbroken, but he also felt guilty, fearing he'd wasted his parents' time and money chasing an impossible dream.

His parents were there to lend support if needed, but Neil kept his feelings of guilt and shame to himself, resulting in him losing his passion for the game. However, despite feeling low, he continued to play football locally, and eventually attracted interest from other professional clubs. He chose to join League One side Wrexham, because it was closest to home.

After a short time there, Neil's love for the game returned. More importantly, so did his confidence. In July of 2007, he signed his first professional contract, making his first-team debut at the age of 18.

To start with, life as a full-time footballer was fun. But professional football is a job, and pretty soon the reality began to sink in. It was all about discipline, hard work, and total commitment. As a youngster, Neil had little freedom, even less glamour, and had the constant pressure of being judged because football is so competitive.

But Neil had a dream, and with patience it began to come true. After making 75 appearances for Wrexham, he moved to Swansea City and then Aston Villa. He was also part of the Great Britain squad at the 2012 Summer Olympics, and capped by the Welsh national team, a huge honour that included making it to the semi-finals of the 2016 Euros.

Now in the latter stages of his playing career, Neil believes that you have to be prepared to step outside your comfort zone to achieve your dream. You also have to embrace change if it helps you towards your goals. Balancing your sporting ambitions with your studies is also essential as you can never be sure your dreams will come true.

A LESSON TO SUPPORT GOOD MENTAL HEALTH: 'The more you learn to adapt, the more rounded as a person you can become.'

Questions to Think About:

1. How is having a schedule helpful in balancing life's responsibilities and hobbies?

2. Neil was always busy with school and sports but made sure to go to bed at the same time after training. Why is sleep important to school and sports performance? How many hours of sleep do you get a night? Do you think you need more or less?

3. Neil avoided talking to trusted family and friends about being released as a player. How do you think it affected his ability to perform well on a day-to-day basis?

4. As a young person trying to work towards a goal, having support is huge. How did parental support help Neil fulfil his dream?

What are this person's signature strengths? How do you know? Provide evidence from the text.

How do you feel after reading the story of this person's life?

PAV SINGH

Supporting, guiding, and empowering others

Pav Singh was living the dream. As a promising youth player at Bradford City Football Club, he was in the elite group of boys with a chance of making a career in professional football. But suddenly it all fell apart when he suffered a badly broken leg.

Pav's football dream appeared to be over, and his father suggested he'd have to face reality. To make a living, he needed to find a new career path. But football had been his life, and his passion for the game was unchanged. He was young and still had the desire and determination to stay in the sport. And with all the knowledge he'd gained during his short playing career, he felt sure he had something of value to offer. The burning question, of course, was what?

At the time, there weren't many South Asian role models in English sport, but there were a few. For example, Ikram Butt had become the first South Asian to play professional rugby league and even went on to play for England.

So, there was some hope. And encouraged by one of his old bosses, Mick Hennigan of Harrogate Town FC, Pav decided to find a way to stay involved.

He examined his strengths. He decided he enjoyed motivating people and was good at communicating his thoughts. He wanted to support and guide players and coaches, empower teams, and strengthen the bond within football clubs so that everyone could become the best they could be.

But first, he had to gain experience. So, to achieve his goal, he took on several jobs in the sports industry. Eventually, he'd end up lecturing in sports coaching and performance. He was a sports development manager and spent time as a football development officer and an academy coach at Leeds United and Bradford City FC.

Pav worked with coaches of all levels and backgrounds, learning the best way of doing the job effectively. He worked hard, helping them in the classroom and out on the field.

Football is ever-changing, and Pav was a student of the game. He was hungry for knowledge and willing to pass that knowledge on whenever he could. 'It's my calling,' he says. 'And certainly part of my DNA.'

Now an experienced coach, he believes, as coach developer, it's important to share the knowledge you have to help others grow, while always being open to admitting what you don't know. He says not knowing something is OK, as you can always find out by asking questions and researching.

Every job has its challenges, and Pav had to spend a lot of time away from his family to pursue his dream. But the support of those closest to him did make his choices a lot easier.

He puts some of his success down to being able to avoid negative situations and people. He also focuses more on solutions than problems. This, he says, is the key to good mental health and wellness for everyone.

Pav says taking time to think about what you're doing and how you're doing it is essential, as it helps you decide what to do next.

Taking time out to reflect can help you come up with different solutions and new ideas that will lead to improvements in how you perform and interact with people.

A LESSON TO SUPPORT GOOD MENTAL HEALTH: 'Be active by taking walks and doing exercise on your own or with family and friends. Exercise can help clear your mind so that you can clearly focus on your next steps.'

Questions to Think About:

1. Pav held many different sports-related jobs to gain experience. What skills do you think Pav developed in these roles that helped him as a coach developer?

2. Having the people who support you nearby is useful to having a healthy mental mind. What can you do to keep connected with friends and family when you are travelling, attending a new school, or even moving home?

3. Pav believes in the importance of focusing on the solution instead of the problem: what does that mean? What can you do to help you develop a solution-focused mindset?

4. How do you think Pav's experience as a player helped him become a better coach developer?

What are this person's signature strengths? How do you know? Provide evidence from the text.

How do you feel after reading the story of this person's life?

RESHMIN CHOWDHURY

Being able to speak different languages to open up a variety of opportunities

As a reporter, the live-shot is one of the most challenging parts of the job. Standing in front of a camera, often in crowded, stressful situations with all eyes upon you, there is nowhere to hide.

Reshmin Chowdhury puts her heart and soul into making sure she gets it right every time. As a journalist and broadcaster, Reshmin has an impressive resume spanning BT Sport, TalkSport and the BBC.

During her career, the British-Asian journalist has worked on an impressive array of top sporting events, including live coverage of the Premier League, Champions League and Europa League, the 2012 Summer Olympics, the 2016 Paralympics, the 2018 FIFA World Cup, and the Women's World Cup in 2019.

Born in London, England, Reshmin grew up in an open-minded Bengali Muslim family. Education, culture, religion, and music played a large role in her upbringing, as did football.

She was especially fascinated by the reporters and presenters who hosted the games. From an early age, she decided that sports broadcast journalism was what she wanted to do.

She chose to study Politics and Economics at the University of Bath, then went to Harlow College to get an NCTJ Post-Graduate Diploma in Newspaper Journalism.

With a good education and solid grounding in media, Reshmin was ready to chase her sporting dream. However, her research told her that you sometimes have to take a roundabout route to achieve your goals. So she joined a news department.

Working as a news assistant, producer, and reporter, she gained a tremendous amount of experience. She also got to travel and practise her language skills.

Being able to speak English, Bengali, French, and Spanish allowed her to connect and build relationships with a wide variety of people. And that would stand her in good stead as her career progressed.

Looking for an opening in sports, Reshmin found a job in Spain working for Real Madrid TV. Moving to a new country meant that she had to adapt to a new way of life. But thanks to her language skills and love of international culture, she rose to the challenge.

However, though Reshmin did her best to join in and embrace all things Spanish, she still held on to her identity. And as a Muslim woman in Spain, she feels that she also helped the locals get a better understanding of her culture.

On match day, she'd be pitch-side at the stadium, doing pre-match interviews and reports, which once again demanded that she had researched as much as possible about the teams to ensure she sounded knowledgeable.

During the game, Reshmin made notes to prepare for the post-match interviews. Football is a global game, and the players come from everywhere. So being able to interview famous footballers in their native tongue was a huge bonus.

Her advice to those who want to follow in her footsteps is to be upbeat and optimistic. She believes you must seize every opportunity to learn and grow.

Stepping out of your comfort zone can be scary, and failures will happen. But she says it's vital to challenge yourself and be unafraid of taking risks.

She encourages young people to be flexible, resourceful, hardworking, resilient, and humble. Working in the media is not easy, but she believes meditation and prayer can help keep your mind clear and release anxiety.

A LESSON TO SUPPORT GOOD MENTAL HEALTH: 'Writing a gratitude journal helps you to appreciate things that will naturally help you to become more grateful. It is important to be thankful and appreciate the kindness of others.'

Questions to Think About:

1. Reshmin says to be humble in the way you work. What does it mean to be humble? Can you give an example of when you have been humble and why?

2. Not only can Reshmin speak in other languages, she can also understand them. How could this help her on the field on match day?

3. Reshmin enjoys experiencing different cultures and integrating into new environments. Why is it important to learn about different people and cultures? What can you do to help you manage in new environments?

4. What key skills does Reshmin need to report on live TV? Do you think her practice of meditation and prayer helps?

What are this person's signature strengths? How do you know? Provide evidence from the text.

How do you feel after reading the story of this person's life?

RIANA SOOBADOO

Facing the challenge of a move abroad

'Are you interested in doing some filming with David Beckham for a new book and video he's releasing?' asked the scout.

Riana was speechless. The man might as well have said, 'Would you like to join our mission to Mars?' for all the sense it made. But this was real! She, Riana Soobadoo of Barnet Ladies in the Women's National League, was being asked to take part in a film shoot with one of her heroes and a football legend. Breathlessly, she accepted.

Co-starring with Becks would be a long way from Riana's humble beginnings in football when she was a young girl training with a local boys' team. Born in London and of Mauritian descent, she got into the game after watching her dad manage a Sunday league side. From there, she began following matches on TV, and at the age of ten, she joined the youth set-up at Arsenal Ladies. She'd been bitten by the football bug and wanted to make the game her life.

The midfielder spent two years with the Gunners, then moved across

London to Leyton Orient, where she captained the O's youth teams for four years. Leaving Orient, she stepped up a level to join Barnet Ladies. There she became the club's youngest-ever first-team player, scoring a hat-trick on her debut and later representing England at under-16 level.

Riana was making her dream a reality. Then, at 18 she got some even more exciting news. She was named the winner of the British Asian Sports Personality of the Year award and was invited to take up a scholarship to study and play football in the United States.

At the time, American college soccer was a breeding ground for many of the game's top female players, including world champions. And though Riana knew that leaving her family and friends to go to the USA would be tough, she was determined to take another step on the ladder of success.

So it was that she found herself at St Edward's University in Austin, Texas. The move was a challenge, with a level of commitment that initially came as a shock. Student-athletes in the USA have a heavy workload on the field and in the classroom, but she got used to the pressure and thrived.

After four years in the US, Riana returned to the UK, where she signed for Spurs Ladies, spending four years with Tottenham before taking a break to have a child and focus on being a parent.

Being a first-time mum was a joy, but Riana still loved football. And once she had motherhood under control, her passion for the game pulled her back in. So she put her boots back on and signed for Cheshunt FC.

For Riana, football goes far beyond what happens on the pitch. She's learned so many valuable life lessons from the game, including teamwork, discipline, commitment, and how to deal with both success and failure. She says she's met some of her best friends through football, and it's also helped her through some tough times.

Riana says if football is what you're passionate about, then work hard, stay focused, and doors will open for you. With many opportunities for women in today's game, in playing, coaching, teaching, or even media, Riana hopes the next generation of females will make an even bigger impact on football than she has done.

A LESSON TO SUPPORT GOOD MENTAL HEALTH: 'Team sport has a way of bringing people together. You can make friends, feel good about yourself, and let off steam. Find something that you love and are passionate about.'

Questions to Think About:

1. What else can teach you discipline and commitment outside of a team sport? Why are these skills important in life?

2. Riana found that moving to America was initially a shock. What challenges did she face? What would you do to prepare yourself to cope away from your family?

3. Riana returned to football after having her first child. How do you think she manages her time, being a mum and a footballer? Try to create her weekly schedule, which includes taking care of her child, training, and games.

4. If you could spend time with a celebrity 'hero' of yours, who would it be? What would you ask them?

What are this person's signature strengths? How do you know? Provide evidence from the text.

How do you feel after reading the story of this person's life?

RITEESH MISHRA

Overcoming injury and rebuilding confidence

There's a saying in sport that achieving success is 90 per cent mental and ten per cent physical. And in football, there's no bigger mental challenge than trying to bounce back from a severe injury.

As a British Indian, Riteesh Mishra was on his way to the top as a youth player at Nottingham Forest FC. But with just one tackle, his dreams of stardom came crashing down.

During an academy game with Leeds United, Riteesh suffered a horrendous double leg fracture, which put him on the sidelines for months. Once the injury healed, he worked hard with the club physio trying to get back to fitness. But the damage wasn't just physical.

'Mentally, I wasn't in a good place,' he says. 'But you can't show any weakness. I couldn't go to a coach and say, "I feel like I don't want to be here. I feel worthless." I couldn't say it to my physio either – what if he reported it back to the coaching staff? My family had never been involved in elite sport, so even they didn't really understand what I was going through. I felt like I was on my own.'

Hiding his feelings, Riteesh eventually fought back to fitness. However, his confidence didn't return. He no longer felt like the player he had been. Mentally, he just didn't believe in himself.

The situation was made worse by the fact that Nottingham Forest had changed their manager while he was injured and had gotten rid of their under-23 team. There was nowhere for him to go.

Riteesh feared his football career was over. And when Forest released him, it seemed like the end. Then, while attending trials with some clubs in Scotland, he ran across his old Nottingham Forest academy coach, Michael Jolley.

Riteesh ended up at the University of Stirling, where Michael was the head coach. Michael had started a scholarship programme to get players like Riteesh back into football. And it was there that he really developed his interest in coaching.

Riteesh had a new passion and was inspired to take his coaching badges. In 2016, Riteesh became Head Coach of Charlton Athletic's Women's team, and enjoyed one of his most memorable moments when he got them promoted to the Championship two years later. In 2021, he became Assistant Manager at the club, trailblazing as the most senior South Asian coach in English women's football.

Having come through so many struggles, Riteesh applies the lessons he's learned to his coaching career. He believes honesty between a coach and his players is essential. Being open with each other creates a supportive atmosphere in which you don't have to put on a brave face when you're struggling.

Riteesh loves coaching because he gets to help people become better every day. Watching players improve, building team spirit, creating a positive environment, and getting an edge on the opposition are equally important to him.

Aside from communication, Riteesh believes an essential part of being a coach is the ability to put yourself in a player's shoes. People respond differently to various situations, and a coach must try to understand each personality and what will help them best.

A LESSON TO SUPPORT GOOD MENTAL HEALTH: 'Try and talk to someone and have a balanced way of thinking as life will have highs and lows; you have to find ways of managing that.'

Questions to Think About:

1. Who do you have in your life that you can go to when you need to talk through a problem? What qualities does that person have?

2. Injuries happen and can have an impact on you playing sport. Can you list some strategies that you could use to help you maintain mental toughness when dealing with a challenging time?

3. Empathy is about putting yourself in someone else's shoes. Why is being empathetic important? Can you give an example of when you have demonstrated empathy?

4. What are the ingredients of creating a positive learning environment? Can you explain the benefits of each ingredient?

What are this person's signature strengths? How do you know? Provide evidence from the text.

How do you feel after reading the story of this person's life?

DR ROBINA SHAH, MBE

Using strong leadership to deliver transformative change

Football is more than just a game; it's an industry and a way of life. From the pitch to the boardroom to the terraces, there's a lot to understand. And if you want to be involved in developing the sport, you can never stop learning.

Dr Robina Shah, MBE, has taken on that challenge. She works as a Non-Executive Director of the FA Women's Football Board and Manchester FA Board of Directors. Her goals are summed up in one simple motto: 'Football for all.'

Robina's passion for football began as a child when her father and brothers encouraged her to play and attend games. As a youngster, she relished the teamwork and the struggle to improve each day. Growing up with their support and love transformed her into a passionate member of the football family.

When she became a mum, she gave her football-mad son the same kind of encouragement that she'd enjoyed in her playing days. However, Robina took things a step further.

Inspired by the growing interest in football among girls and women, Dr

Robina decided that she'd like to work in the game. Realising that not all females have the same level of support that she'd had from her family and community, Robina began promoting inclusion in football.

As a medical professional, she'd held several leadership roles in the NHS in which she'd championed equality and diversity. Applying that idea to football, she joined the Women's Football Board, Manchester FA and FA Disability Football Committee. In these roles, Robina believes her job is to help the FA make football more inclusive, accessible, and visible, especially among communities that people believe are hard to reach. Dr Robina has many responsibilities in her different roles. She most enjoys bringing a strategic view of the future of football. This means looking ahead at how everyone can work together for the good of the game.

One of the challenges the game faces is understanding the role football can play in different communities. The FA has a huge platform, with the opportunity to impact communities suffering from issues like cardiovascular disease, isolation, and mental health problems.

Among the things Robina noticed was the lack of women and young people from diverse backgrounds in coaching, refereeing, or volunteer leadership roles. So, staying true to her motto, 'Football for all,' she looks for gaps in those areas and works to fill them with people who are otherwise under-represented in the game.

As well as working to include family carers and people with a disability, Robina is also involved in the FA Heads Up Campaign, which seeks to use football to motivate and inspire conversations about mental health.

As a former player with a supportive network, Dr Robina understands how football can promote mental well-being. It's a stress reliever and also creates a feeling of belonging and being part of a team. Any form of physical activity also stimulates the production of endorphins. These are natural mood lifters that can help keep anxiety and depression at bay. Endorphins may also leave you feeling more relaxed, happy, and optimistic after a hard workout on the pitch! As we know, it's not easy to make football all inclusive, and there are many reasons why it can be a slow process, such as a lack of people, resources, or funding. But Robina believes that with strong leadership, shared purpose, and ambition, changes will happen. And she's committed to leading the change.

Robina feels it's essential to be clear about your role and your expectations to accomplish anything in life. She believes it's vital to work with others and value their contribution as you move toward your goal.

She says you should be confident about what you know, value your voice, and trust your experience. But you can never know everything, so it's important to fill in the gaps in your knowledge by actively learning.

A LESSON TO SUPPORT GOOD MENTAL HEALTH: 'Make time for yourself and understand your limitations. Your physical health is interdependent on your mental health, so looking after yourself is a must.'

Questions to Think About:

1. How do you think playing football helps with your mental health?

2. Can you list three things you can do to support your mental health?

3. Robina believes in 'football for all'. What does this mean to you? Can you be creative and make up your own slogan that places the emphasis on equality?

4. Have you ever felt like you couldn't do or try something that interested you? How did you overcome that?

What are this person's signature strengths? How do you know? Provide evidence from the text.

How do you feel after reading the story of this person's life?

RUPESH POPAT

Finding players to perform at a high level

Rupesh Popat was football mad.

'Football can't be your whole life,' his teacher would say. But Rupesh disagreed.

After finishing his GCSEs at the age of 16 he began to focus more on coaching young kids as a volunteer in his community. He was passionate about it, coaching locally during university, then going on to coach in Africa and the USA after graduating.

His dedication and overseas experience helped build his confidence. And when he returned to the UK, he secured a role coaching the academy players at Fulham Football Club. That would have been enough for many people. But after three years at Fulham, Rupesh needed a new challenge.

Germany beckoned, so he was off on his travels again.

He began by working in the third tier of German football as an assistant coach for the under-21 team of FC Carl Zeiss Jena, where he also assisted the first-team coach and scouted for new talent.

While coaching, Rupesh continued his studies, earning a master's degree in Performance Analysis at a Cologne sports university. He was building a good resume, and in 2020, he made two major breakthroughs. In January, he secured a part-time job as a first-team video scout with the English Championship side, Millwall. A month later, he got an internship as a youth scout for the Academy Recruitment department of the famous Bundesliga club, Werder Bremen.

Rupesh has to watch a lot of football matches, live and on video. His job is to spot players who have the skills, style, and attitude that fit the club he's working for. It's rather like a treasure hunt, in which Rupesh is searching for an uncut diamond that the coaches at the club can polish into a first-team player or even a shining star.

Of course, to uncover a gem, Rupesh has to sift through a ton of rocks, often in places where other people won't look. But it's a part of the job he enjoys. Discovering a player with the potential to compete at a higher level is hugely satisfying. It's also a great skill.

Naturally, the job does have its challenges. As a scout, you have to be in the know, which means you need a network of contacts within the game who can alert you to a player who might be worth looking at. Developing those relationships takes time and effort. You have to give as much as you take, sharing information to build the credibility and trust you need to succeed.

A football club is only as good as its players, so recruitment plays a vital role. To stay on top of the job, Rupesh says you can never stop being a student. That means he's always ready to learn. Not only does he spend hours watching matches, but he also studies other teams, coaches, and players to gain a better understanding of the game and more awareness of what the most successful clubs are doing.

Aside from perseverance and a willingness to travel, Rupesh got to where he is by becoming a specialist in uncovering talent that's been missed. And he believes that's important. With whatever path you take in football, it's easier to stand out if you can add value to a club by offering skills and expertise they don't already have.

A LESSON TO SUPPORT GOOD MENTAL HEALTH: 'Develop relationships and friendships with positive and trustworthy people who care about your well-being and encourage you to pursue your dreams. They are your personal fan club. They will lift you back up when you are down.'

Questions to Think About:

1. Rupesh used his passion to help him find a way of working in football. What are you passionate about and why?

2. Travelling to gain well-rounded experience has helped Rupesh in his career. What are the benefits of travelling and visiting different places?

3. Rupesh believes having a particular area of strength can be a huge advantage. Think of a long-term goal that you are interested in. What could you do to help you achieve this?

4. Developing relationships and friendships takes time and effort. What did Rupesh do to gain credibility and develop friendships and relationships?

What are this person's signature strengths? How do you know? Provide evidence from the text.

How do you feel after reading the story of this person's life?

RUPINDER BAINS

Becoming the first South Asian to be appointed to the Board at the FA

Self-doubt goes with the territory when you're ambitious. Even the most confident person may have a private moment when they wonder whether they're up to the task. Such a moment came for Rupinder Bains when she became the first South Asian and Sikh woman to be appointed to the board of the English Football Association.

Anybody would be honoured and a little scared to join the organisation.

And, as a non-executive director, Rupinder was no exception. Would her experience be respected? As an Asian woman, would her voice be heard in a traditionally white, mostly male environment? As a board member, she was joining a team that aims to make football a better experience for everyone. Could she do the job?

Rupinder's first experience in professional football came when she worked as a lawyer for Peterborough United. Working for the chairman and the fantastic management team, she found football a complex but fascinating challenge. Soon, her law firm began representing several other football clubs, allowing Rupinder to get some valuable experience into how the business of football works.

Rupinder met people involved in many areas of the game. As she developed relationships with other professionals, her star began to rise. Eventually, she found herself at the top, as the first Asian member of the FA board.

As a board member, she helps to make crucial decisions on many aspects of football, from events on the pitch to commercial contracts to strategy development, and more.

Rupinder says the most enjoyable part of her role is that she can make a real difference to the game. Of course, the decision-making process can be slow, and it can take a while to get things done. But she believes there's a real desire for change at all levels of the game, especially when it comes to diversity and inclusion, and she's glad to be among those making it happen.

Sadly, Rupinder has encountered some racism during her career. One incident happened early on at a large London law firm, where she was made to feel like an outsider, even though she was born and raised in London.

Naturally, experiencing discrimination of any kind is a horrible feeling. However, Rupinder decided she would not allow her gender or skin colour to dictate what she could or could not achieve. Instead, she stood up for herself, displaying honesty, confidence, and a willingness to work hard. She's now the Managing Director of a law firm with her business partner, John Spyrou. And together they enjoy running a diverse and inclusive business.

The single, most valuable piece of advice Rupinder can offer is to network. Build strong relationships and let those within your networks know about your ambitions. What are your dreams? Whatever they are, they'll stay as dreams if you keep them to yourself. Without being too pushy or self-centred, you have to advertise yourself as you never know who might be willing to open an important door.

Rupinder believes people should have the chance to talk about their feelings with others. Trust and honesty are vital. There should be no shame around the subject of mental health either. Everyone needs to know that it's OK not to be OK sometimes.

A LESSON TO SUPPORT GOOD MENTAL HEALTH: 'Talk. Express your worries and conerns; do not bottle them up. Talking about how you feel can lead to good healthy minds.'

Questions to Think About:

1. Rupinder was born and raised in London, but sometimes she still felt like an outsider. Why did she feel like this? What would you do if you are made to feel like you do not belong?

2. Research professional footballers who are campaigning to stop racism. Who are they and what are they doing?

3. Talking about feelings can help us overcome stressful situations. Who are some people you can trust and talk to? Who should you avoid talking to about things that are personal?

4. What does it mean when Rupinder says, 'It's OK not to be OK sometimes'?

What are this person's signature strengths? How do you know? Provide evidence from the text.

How do you feel after reading the story of this person's life?

SAAD WADIA

Connecting with people through sport

Saad looked up at the cloudy skies above his new home and shivered. The weather in England was very different from his old home in India. And it wasn't the only thing that was different. Here in the heart of East London, he had to find a way to fit in, to make friends, to do well in his new school. But it wasn't going to be easy.

Saad didn't know at the time, but he had mild dyslexia, and a stutter that appeared when he felt uncomfortable. And here in this foreign country that was new to him, he wasn't comfortable at all! Feeling like he didn't belong, he'd sit in the back of the classroom or in a corner, watching without joining in.

Saad had to work three or four times harder than the other students to produce even average work. But despite his challenges, he persevered and eventually earned a full scholarship to study for a football degree at UCFB, based at Wembley Stadium.

Soon, Saad began to network with people. He volunteered for several organisations, including the HRH Prince? of Wales charity. As his confidence grew, he started volunteering projects in the fashion industry, set up a magazine and started getting involved with marketing in the entertainment world. He was unstoppable, and with hard work and determination, he excelled at university and graduated.

As a kid, Saad's friend, Zulqi Khan, was one of the best local footballers around. In fact, Saad had never understood why Zulqi hadn't been signed by a professional club. That got him thinking. What if he could connect grassroots players to the professional football system? How could he help players find their way to the top of the game?

Saad put his big idea into practice, inspired in part by David Beckham, who grew up in the same area of East London as him, and he started Avalon Sports Management. Currently, Saad manages several former and current top players, guiding their career development on the pitch, and building their brands off it. This includes former Welsh international Ian Rush, MBE, who spent many years playing for Liverpool FC. He also consults for various football clubs and brands, connecting the football and the business world.

One of the things Saad really enjoys is seeing people grow in the industry.

He feels that sports allow you to give back and connect to people like nothing else, and many of his clients have expanded their reach to fans around the world.

Saad overcame his shyness and began his career at an early age. He had no experience but did have something unique to bring to the table. There aren't many Indian role models in the professional football world, but he didn't let that deter him. His focus was on being the best that he could be.

Of course, it wasn't all smooth sailing, and Saad had many failures. But he always took something from every disappointment. He believes failure is an opportunity to learn and try again.

Saad wants young people to know that the sports industry has a broad range of opportunities. He advises them to take their time and work to understand the business from all angles. Football is a competitive industry, so you need to make sure you're enthusiastic and always looking to improve your knowledge and add value.

A LESSON TO SUPPORT GOOD MENTAL HEALTH: 'You should always have a good balance of mental, physical and spiritual health. Life can be fast paced and you can get lost sometimes, so it's always important to keep focused and take it one step at a time. Always remember to go at your own pace, as everyone's journey is different.'

Questions to Think About:

1. Saad says that it is important to go at your own pace. Why is this important and how will it help your mental health?

2. Saad has mild dyslexia. Can you find out more about dyslexia? How did it make Saad feel and how did he cope with it?

3. Saad was once very shy at school and now he regularly must communicate with a variety of people. How does having good people skills help you in school? At home?

4. Saad did not have any mentors to look up to. Do you think it is necessary to have someone to look up to? Explain your answer.

What are this person's signature strengths? How do you know? Provide evidence from the text.

How do you feel after reading the story of this person's life?

SABAH MAHMOOD

Standing up for your cultural identity within sport

It's fair to say that football has never been more aware of its image than it is now, especially when it comes to racism.

British-Pakistani footballer, Sabah Mahmood, began her football journey in East London, where her school PE teacher was the first to encourage and support her dreams.

At the age of 17 Sabah was good enough to start playing in the Essex County Women's League. Though she still wore a hijab to play, she was keen to break down stereotypes about Asian women. However, it was not a happy experience as the atmosphere was toxic. Sabah was frequently targeted for abuse. Players would try to injure her or make spiteful remarks to shake her confidence and emotions. Girls would comment about her South Asian heritage, make fun of her Muslim beliefs, and mock her hijab.

Sabah felt utterly alone, and the pressure of being judged and made to feel inferior weighed heavily on her mind. After a season, she'd had enough and decided to quit the team.

But Sabah was too strong to give up on football completely. She was determined to find her place in the game, not only as a player but also as an example to other young women with a similar sporting passion. And so, with the support of her sisters and friends, she continued to play, enjoying regular kickabouts at university. Eventually, with her confidence restored, she decided she was ready to play for a team again.

Unlike before, Sabah was welcomed and accepted. She made new friends and enjoyed competing with her teammates. This team was full of supportive cheers and faithful friends.

After a year of playing together, some of the players decided to set-up an 11-a-side team called London Bari Women FC. Sabah was thrilled, and took on the role of team captain and club secretary. The London Bari team was an immediate success, finishing fourth in the league and reaching a cup final.

Sabah had grown as a person and a player. And it wasn't long before her talent caught the eye of the National Women's League side, Leyton Orient. Sabah signed up and looked forward to a bright career. But sadly, it would be blighted by an injury from which she couldn't fully recover.

For some people, that would be where the dream ended. But once again, Sabah refused to give up. Instead, she wanted to use her experiences to help the next generation of female footballers and become a coach.

Though she experienced more than her fair share of racism because of her heritage and skin colour, Sabah believes that sport has the power to create unity and equality for all. As a youngster, she faced family and cultural opposition to her football dreams, whereas nowadays she feels it's becoming more acceptable for young Asian girls to play sports.

Sabah's message to young people is to stay brave and be strong. Never be afraid to aim high and want more from yourself no matter what path you follow in football or life. Always be proud of your identity and who you are.

Of course, there may be many obstacles along the way. But when it comes to football, you should never forget that it's called 'the beautiful game' and you're meant to play it with a smile.

A LESSON TO SUPPORT GOOD MENTAL HEALTH: 'Never give up. The longer you keep moving in the right direction, the closer you will get to your goal – so do not stop!'

Questions to Think About:

1. Sabah experienced racism when she was playing football. How do you think this made her feel? What could you do if you saw a classmate or teammate being racist to someone?

2. Why is it important to surround yourself with supportive and positive people?

3. How could Sabah's challenging experiences help her? Can you think of a tough time that helped you change or grow in some way?

4. There are more girls and women playing football or taking up a job in the sport. Do you think girls are given the same opportunities as boys in sport? Explain your answer.

What are this person's signature strengths? How do you know? Provide evidence from the text.

How do you feel after reading the story of this person's life?

SABRINA DALE

Constantly having to prove herself

Football was Sabrina's passion, whether playing outside with the neighbourhood boys, watching Football Italia, or memorising every player's stats in a World Cup Superstars book. A football environment was where she belonged.

Before too long, she was turning up to play with Punjab United in Gravesend, Kent, where the voices of doubt and disapproval she'd heard from her family were drowned out by her coach's encouraging words. For the first time in her life, somebody recognised her talent. Sabrina felt unstoppable!

There's an old saying that goes, 'Do what you love, and you'll never work a day in your life.' And Sabrina took this to heart. She loved sport, so she took a degree in Sport and Exercise and became a primary school sports coach. It was rewarding work, and she liked nothing better than seeing a child enjoying a sport they'd never tried before.

Beyond her day job, Sabrina was also coaching football, offering her know-how to several different clubs, including Punjab United.

Coming from a South Asian background where many in the older generation thought girls shouldn't play football, Sabrina was committed to helping kids like her who wanted to play the game. So, she focused her efforts on coaching girls' teams.

Her first big coaching role was with the girls' team at Coventry City FC. Naturally, she was nervous, but the squad's talent and eagerness soon got rid of her jitters. It was a great team to coach, and the players brought out the best in her. After honing her skills with Coventry, Sabrina went searching for a manager's job. She found one at Sporting Khalsa, a Midlands League club where she took charge of the girls' under-16 team. In her first season, Sabrina was both successful and popular. She'd eventually go on to coach the under-18 team and get her UEFA B coaching licence.

Unafraid of hard work, Sabrina also took on the job of women's coach at Saltley Stallions FC, a club that supports young players from underprivileged backgrounds. Just like her, many grew up being told what to do with their lives. Now, they're doing exactly what they want to do, and Sabrina loves to see them learning and enjoying themselves.

Sabrina feels she faced her biggest challenges during childhood, trying to prove she could make football her life. In a male-dominated sport, she encountered some resistance. People underestimated her, assuming she didn't know much about the game because she was a woman.

But Sabrina took it all in her stride and got on with the job at hand, continuing to develop her skills and knowledge, now combining football with sport psychology.

Sabrina says it's about doing the best she can for the people and players she works with. Her advice is never to stop growing and learning. Find experienced people to advise you and learn from them. Stay in touch with friends in the game, as a network is important for finding support and new opportunities.

Sabrina says you have to understand that everyone is on their own journey and wants different things from their coaching or playing career. Sport doesn't always need to be a competition. Do things at your own pace, and when you are ready, then that's when the time is right.

A LESSON TO SUPPORT GOOD MENTAL HEALTH: 'Sometimes things might seem overwhelming, but that is OK. Believe in yourself, speak to others around you, and you will get there. Enjoy the process!'

Questions to Think About:

1. Sabrina is a huge believer in being true to yourself. What does that mean? How can you stay true to yourself?

2. What does it mean not to focus on your ego? How can your ego get in the way of your success?

3. Sabrina loves to coach girls and children, helping them discover something they love to do. Who has helped you discover something you love to do?

4. As a sports psychologist, Sabrina works with players to help them develop a healthy mind. What can you do to keep a healthy mind, and why is this important?

What are this person's signature strengths? How do you know? Provide evidence from the text.

How do you feel after reading the story of this person's life?

SEEMA JASWAL

Becoming the face of football in India

The title music plays. You shuffle your papers one last time. You hear the assistant director counting down in your earpiece. Fixing your eyes on the camera, a smile at the ready, you wait for the studio floor manager's cue to start speaking. You're the face of football for millions, and there's no better feeling in the world.

Seema Jaswal is living the dream. As the host of the Premier League's global *Match Day Live* coverage and ITV's international football shows, she's an award-winning TV presenter with the world at her feet.

Putting on a live football broadcast takes a vast team in the studio and at the venues where the matches are played. But the coverage is only as good as the presenter.

Preparation is key, and Seema's job is to be a multi-tasker who's ready for anything. She needs to be a student of the sport she's covering, with detailed knowledge of the rules, the history, the news, the statistics, and the personalities that make up the beautiful game.

She needs to be inquisitive and a great listener, with a sharp mind that's able to come up with the ideal phrase or the perfect interview question at just the right time. And she has to be likeable and fun, to bring the best out of her guests and ensure that the show is a great experience for the viewers.

Seema's route to the top was not a traditional one. Though she excelled as a youngster in tennis, netball, and table tennis, she didn't study sports journalism or media. Instead, she took a degree in Sociology and Politics at a university in London. But her passion for sport never left her.

Seema eventually became a tennis coach, and when the chance arose to present BBC's *Sportsround* and *Match of the Day Kickabout* on children's television, she jumped at it, even though she had no training.

While working at the BBC, Seema heard that Star Sports was looking for a presenter to host their new Indian Super League coverage. Though nervous, she applied, and to her surprise, she got the job. So, in 2015, she boarded a plane to Mumbai to become the face of Indian football.

Despite her work with the ISL, Seema had a tough time finding other presenting roles. Sports journalism is a highly competitive field, and rejection is common. But she chose to see every disappointment as an inspiration, believing it was all a matter of timing, and her time would come.

Eventually, by remaining upbeat, believing in herself, working hard, and having the courage to dream, Seema achieved her goal. She's since gone on to host various major sporting events, including the 2018 FIFA World Cup, the 2020 UEFA Champions League, and the 2021 Rugby League World Cup Draw at Buckingham Palace.

Seema's advice to anyone wanting to work in football is to dream big and dedicate yourself to understanding the game. She says you need to trust people and be ready to learn from them. And that means asking questions. Because there are no silly questions, and the more you ask, the more you'll know.

A LESSON TO SUPPORT GOOD MENTAL HEALTH: 'You're never alone. Always reach out and talk about how you feel, you'll be surprised by how much love the world has to give you. Everyone faces challenges in their lives and they all come in different shapes and sizes. Remember you are special and you never have to go through anything alone.'

Questions to Think About:

1. Seema did not get a degree in journalism, but still achieved her dream. Imagine your dream job, then write down three different ways you could try to achieve that.

2. Live TV is stressful! What do you think you could do to be ready to be interviewed? This might be for a school or job. What feelings might you experience? What can you do to manage stress?

3. Seema says, 'There is never a silly question' – what does she mean and why is asking questions important?

4. Besides knowing a lot about football – how else do you think Seema prepares for her job?

What are this person's signature strengths? How do you know? Provide evidence from the text.

How do you feel after reading the story of this person's life?

SUKI TONKS

Creating diverse leadership boards

Suki was born into an athletic South Asian family. Football was a big part of family life, and Suki gave as good as she got when it came to kickabouts with her brothers. She was determined, tough, and fast.

Many people said Suki should get serious about the game and try to become a footballer. But strangely, though she had natural talent and grit, she lacked confidence. She worried she wouldn't be good enough, and didn't quite believe that football was for girls.

Suki's playing career was over before it had even begun. She eventually became a lawyer, though she remained a football fan in her spare time. Years later, as a wife and mother, Suki would cheer from the touchline whenever her football-loving husband and sons played for their local teams. But it wasn't until her daughter wanted to play that Suki decided it was time to get more involved in the game.

Recalling the fears that ended her football ambitions, Suki set about encouraging her daughter and other girls to believe in their abilities. Football is known as a game for all, and Suki wanted to show that girls are just as entitled to follow their football dreams as boys.

In January 2020, Suki became a non-executive director at Nottingham Forest Women's Football Club. A non-executive director helps the club make decisions, plan, and write policies. She's also a member of The Football Association's National Asian Women in Football Advisory Group. Her role at Forest allows her to have a real impact on the women's game by encouraging equality, diversity, and inclusion.

Though Suki hasn't been closely involved in football all her life, her contribution is valuable. Looking at the game with a fresh pair of eyes can help her spot issues more experienced people might miss because they're so familiar with how things have always been done.

Admittedly, Suki struggled to understand the business of football early on. The way the different levels work within a club and the football authorities can be complicated and confusing. And the politics of the game are a minefield. But her determination to learn and her will to win shone through.

Working alongside the club chairman, the head coach, and UEFA board members, Suki has been able to help the club make good decisions when it comes to opening up the game to everyone, including members of the Black, Asian, and Minority Ethnic community.

Suki's views are always listened to, respected, and explored. Everyone at Nottingham Forest seems to enjoy working with her, and she hasn't faced any discrimination or ignorance from anyone at the club.

Suki believes that people shouldn't hesitate to apply for leadership roles in football, even if they've never played the game. When it comes to understanding diversity, life experience can be just as valuable.

Fear stopped Suki from achieving her potential as a player, but off the field she's learned to thrive. She says worrying about what might happen means you're not concentrating on what's actually happening.

Winners are present in the moment, giving 100 per cent right there and then. And that kind of mindfulness, she believes, is the best way to be successful and effective.

A LESSON TO SUPPORT GOOD MENTAL HEALTH: 'Take each day as it comes – we cannot control most of the external factors that lead to anxiety, but we can control how we choose to deal with these factors.'

Questions to Think About:

1. Suki was inspired to work in football when her daughter decided to play. How do you think that helped her daughter's experience? How did that decision help Suki?

2. Even though she did not face discrimination in her position, what challenges did Suki overcome? How did she overcome them?

3. Have you overcome a challenge in your life? What was the challenge and what did you do?

4. Suki wants you to practise mindfulness and being present. What does this mean to you? What helps you relax and refocus when your mind begins to worry?

What are this person's signature strengths? How do you know? Provide evidence from the text.

How do you feel after reading the story of this person's life?

VANISHA PATEL

Inspiring the next generation

It was a sunny afternoon at her primary school in Kent, England, when Vanisha Patel stumbled upon the game that changed her life. While watching some boys having a kickabout on the field, she was asked to join in. For a laugh, she agreed. And to their surprise and hers, she was pretty good.

As luck would have it, one of the boys said his father coached a local football team. She was invited to try out. And soon Vanisha signed up.

Over the next year or so, she got better and better. Though most of her teammates were boys, she was a star player and Vanisha began to dream about a football career.

But then, in 2003, her dream was shattered. At the age of 11 she was no longer allowed to play on a team with boys. She was out!

It was a painful setback, but Vanisha was determined to carry on. So she begged her best friend's dad to start a girls' team. He agreed, and at 12 Vanisha became captain of Deal Town Rangers.

The team had great success, winning the local league and cup. That year,

Vanisha was voted player of the season. She also won a national award as Junior Sports Personality of the Year.

The team's success drew the attention of scouts from various London football clubs. Vanisha was invited for trials with Charlton Athletic. At the first two, she wasn't picked. But she swallowed her disappointment and tried again. This time, she was successful and joined the club's under-14 Centre of Excellence.

Playing for Charlton was a tough challenge because it took her three hours to travel from home to the training ground. Thankfully, her parents took her whenever she needed to go.

Battling her way through the ranks at Charlton, she became reserve team captain at 17 and eventually a regular starter for the first team. Her football dream was coming true.

But it wasn't her only ambition. While at Charlton, Vanisha began studying for a teaching degree at Brunel University. Her classes were on the other side of London from the football club. With the pressure of her studies, trekking across town became too much. Vanisha made the hard decision to put her football career on hold.

She returned to the game after getting her first teaching job. This time, she signed for Gillingham Football Club but struggled to get back to fitness. However, with the same determination she'd shown throughout her career, she fought her way into the starting line-up.

Vanisha went on to help Gillingham win promotion to the Southern Premier League. She even captained the side in the following season. But then disaster struck when she tore her ACL – a vital knee ligament.

It was the kind of injury that can end a football career. But once again, Vanisha had the heart to bounce back.

She was supposed to be out for a year. She returned after just nine months. And she didn't let her time on the sidelines go to waste either, as she threw herself into her teaching job, earning several promotions.

Vanisha has now given up playing football to concentrate on teaching. But she hopes her story will inspire the next generation of female players.

A LESSON TO SUPPORT GOOD MENTAL HEALTH: 'Never stop reaching for the stars. Football is a game of opinions; you just need to keep working hard until you find the person who believes in you and takes you to the next level. Don't ever be disheartened, keep believing.'

Questions to Think About:

1. Do you think it was difficult for Vanisha to play on an all-boys' team? What challenges do you think she might have had?

2. Vanisha had to play under pressure when scouts came to watch her and her team. What helpful steps might she have taken to prepare?

3. Vanisha sacrificed her football dream to pursue a career in teaching, and coming back to football was a struggle. What do you think Vanisha felt about herself when struggling to regain her physical fitness? What messages do you tell yourself when you are finding something challenging?

4. Vanisha has said, 'Football is a game of opinions . . .' What do you think she means by that? How would you manage opinions that you disagree with?

What are this person's signature strengths? How do you know? Provide evidence from the text.

How do you feel after reading the story of this person's life?

YASHMIN HARUM, BEM

Making a difference

When Yashmin Harum BEM took her young son to play football, they were both excited.

'You're going to do great!' she whispered as he trotted onto the pitch. But as she looked around, she didn't see many people that looked like her and her son.

As a Bengali-Gujarati, Yashmin is proud of her culture. But living in Britain is not without its challenges. Would her son face any problems? Would he be accepted?

Yashmin decided a change was needed in her community so that more South Asians took up the game. She saw an opportunity to make a difference – and make a difference she did, creating MSA, Muslimah Sports Association, offering women a safe and positive environment to participate in a number of different sports without compromising their religious or cultural beliefs.

Since childhood, Yashmin and her two older brothers had loved football. She had started playing at a young age with her brothers and their friends.

When her family moved to Scotland, she continued to play, though only with the boys in the school playground as there was no girls' team to join.

When Yashmin and her family moved back to London, she eventually attended an all-girls secondary school that had a football team that she immediately joined.

On leaving school, Yashmin decided to skip further education. Instead, she got married and started a career in banking. But football was never far from her mind. She still saw the need for change but knew she had to become one of the influencers to make it happen.

Yashmin enrolled in the PFA's 'On the Board' programme, and the Sporting Equals LeaderBoard Academy, which are designed to help people in the Black, Asian, and Minority Ethnic communities acquire the skills to become leaders and decision-makers in sport.

After completing the courses and a lot of hard work, Yashmin got several board positions. She is the first Asian woman to become an Independent director at British Fencing and to serve on the London FA Council. Her job is to check and challenge the decision-makers, raising issues relevant to minority communities that they may not have considered.

To make football more appealing to groups not generally involved in the game, Yashmin has worked tirelessly to help coaches become qualified to coach young girls and women, creating role models for others to follow. Now, through MSA, Yashmin can offer a variety of sporting experiences for women, in a safe and nurturing environment.

Being a Muslim South Asian woman in football, with no higher education and only a minor sports background, Yashmin has undoubtedly encountered resistance. You have to fight your corner to be heard and accepted. That requires support and the ability to adapt to challenging situations.

It takes drive, knowledge, passion and a position of influence to be taken seriously. That's why Yashmin encourages others to follow in her footsteps.

Her advice is that with each failure, your resilience and character should grow. When you don't meet your goals, you should learn from the experience and reassess the situation. Never give up because setbacks mean you're trying.

Yashmin has come a long way from that nervous mum on the sidelines.

She set out to make a difference, and it's a source of great pride that she's doing just that.

A LESSON TO SUPPORT GOOD MENTAL HEALTH: 'Challenges bring opportunities and you learn more from failure than from success, as failure is success in progress.'

Questions to Think About:

1. Yashmin showed us you don't have to have a university degree to effect change in football. What did she do to help her achieve her goals?

2. What does it mean that Yashmin's job is to 'check and challenge' the board members? How could you apply this strategy to help you?

3. When Yashmin took her son to play football, she noticed that there were not many people that looked like her. What would you do in this situation? Why?

4. What things motivate you to be successful and why?

What are this person's signature strengths? How do you know? Provide evidence from the text.

How do you feel after reading the story of this person's life?

YASMIN SAEED

Remaining focused after a career-ending challenge

Yasmin Saeed was born with football in her blood. Her mum was a player, and even as a toddler, Yasmin would cheer her on from the sidelines.

At the age of four, Yasmin began playing for a local boys' team. Before too long, she was on the radar of professional club scouts. She eventually signed for Manchester United Ladies, before moving on to play for Crewe Alexandra, Manchester City, and Everton.

At Everton, things looked bright for the 15-year-old, but then disaster struck. During a tough game, Yasmin fell to the ground in agony. Curled up in a ball on the grass, the teenager had no idea that her playing career was over, but it was. She'd suffered a fractured pelvis.

She felt that everything she'd worked towards as a footballer was for nothing. Her body would never be strong enough to play again. In fact, she'd spend months in the hospital relearning how to walk.

During her treatment, she got talking to a fellow patient whose dad was a football referee. They spoke about the games he handled and what it was like to be the man in the middle. That got Yasmin thinking. If she couldn't *play* football any more, perhaps she could become a ref?

Happily, Yasmin was eventually able to walk and run again. And once she'd recovered, she began taking courses in football refereeing. Although this is changing, compared to men there are very few female referees at any level of the game, and even fewer with a South Asian background. But Yasmin was determined and quickly climbed the ranks.

By the age of 19 she was a semi-professional ref, whose knowledge of the game and refereeing skills had her tipped for the top. One of her first career highlights was working as an assistant referee at England's National Training Centre, where she ran the line during an under-15 international between England and Scotland. She currently referees both men's and women's games, and has her sights set on becoming the first female referee to take charge of a Premier League game.

Yasmin says being a ref is a huge buzz, especially when thousands of people are watching. She believes staying calm under pressure, and standing firm on her decisions is the key, not only in football but also in life.

During her career, she's had the opportunity to meet and connect with a wide range of people from different backgrounds and cultures. For example, in 2018, she represented the English Football Association in Belgium at an event called 'The Premier League Remembers Tournament', which commemorated World War Two.

Yasmin faces many challenges as a referee, both as a female and as a mixed-race person. Dealing with ignorance, sexism and racism is tough. But Yasmin has never been discouraged by the negativity of others, and instead focuses on being the best that she can be. She believes she deserves to be treated as an equal, regardless of her gender or culture. And that means on the field and off it.

Yasmin says you should never give up on your dreams. Work hard and enjoy the rewards that follow. She says refereeing is a wonderful job, and she'd love to see more girls taking it up.

A LESSON TO SUPPORT GOOD MENTAL HEALTH: 'Learn and grow from your experiences and remember to talk to someone if you are struggling with any big feelings. Sharing how you feel will make you feel better.'

Questions to Think About:

1. Think about Yasmin after her injury – what habits or characteristics did she have in place to help her through that challenge?

2. Yasmin graduated in Sports Psychology. Find out more about this subject and write about what you have learned.

3. How did being a player help Yasmin become an efficient and fair referee?

4. Have you ever dealt with sexism or racism? How did you respond? What steps would you take to ensure someone else's opinion does not affect how you think about yourself?

What are this person's signature strengths? How do you know? Provide evidence from the text.

How do you feel after reading the story of this person's life?

DR ZAFAR IQBAL

Helping players return to what they enjoy doing

Sometimes in life, triumph is born out of tragedy. Growing up, Zafar Iqbal, known as 'Zaf', watched helplessly as his younger sister battled brain cancer. As anyone who's dealt with the illness of a loved one will know, it can be confusing and frustrating. You want to help, but what can you do?

Obviously, as a child, kind words were all that Zaf could offer. But he knew that he wanted to do more when he grew up, which set him on the path towards becoming a doctor.

In his youth, Zaf fell victim to the footballers' curse – a damaged anterior cruciate ligament, or ACL, which is the ligament that keeps your knee stable. The injury is common among footballers and, sadly, has ended the careers of many professional players.

As an amateur footballer, the injury was not career-ending, but the treatment he received in the hospital did change Zaf's career path and he decided to switch the focus of his studies to sports medicine.

After completing university, Dr Zaf began combining his work in various

NHS and private sports medicine clinics with voluntary work in different sports.

In 2005, he started working with Leyton Orient Football Club and at the England FA youth training camps. Two years later, he became the Academy Doctor at Tottenham Hotspur FC and the following year was appointed as the First Team Doctor.

After three years at Spurs, he moved to Liverpool FC, where he worked as the Head of Sports Medicine for five seasons before heading back to London to become Head of Sports Medicine at Crystal Palace Football Club.

Dr Zaf's job is to take responsibility for the health and welfare of the players. He sees the treatment of an injured player as a puzzle to be solved. He tries to understand their health, history, goals, weaknesses, and strengths. Armed with that information, he can devise a plan to help them regain their fitness as quickly as possible and maintain it long-term.

Dr Zaf says he loves the challenge of helping athletes get back to doing what they do best – competing at the highest level.

Like many successful people, Dr Zaf believes there is no substitute for hard work and sacrifice. His parents made huge sacrifices to enable him to go to university, and his wife has taken prolonged career breaks to allow him to continue working in sports medicine.

Some key advice that he offers to young people is not to chase the money but to seek out a job that you love. He says you should make decisions based on facts, not emotions, and should never stop learning.

The biggest challenge is balancing family life with the needs of the players and the club. Finding that balance takes practice and patience. Dr Zaf also feels being true to yourself is very important.

As a Muslim, Dr Zaf has to ensure that he is able to practise his religion in his workplace. And club officials at Crystal Palace do their best to help. During Ramadan, for example, they make sure he has a separate Sehri meal brought to his room when travelling away. Actions like that help him feel comfortable and respected as an employee from a different culture in a game that belongs to the world.

A LESSON TO SUPPORT GOOD MENTAL HEALTH: 'Working in football is very intense and never stops. With whatever you do, you need to make sure that you look after yourself and don't allow it to overwhelm you.'

Questions to Think About:

1. Dr Zaf Iqbal talked about sacrifice being important to success. What can you sacrifice in your daily routine to help you succeed in your goals?

2. What does he mean when he advises someone 'not to chase the money' and to 'seek out a job that you love'? What would be your ideal job and why?

3. Why is it important not to make decisions when you are emotional? List three things that you can do to help you regulate your emotions.

4. The club makes sure that Dr Zaf has a separate Sehri meal during Ramadan. What is a Sehri meal? Can you find out more about Ramadan and how Muslim athletes prepare during this holy month?

What are this person's signature strengths? How do you know? Provide evidence from the text.

How do you feel after reading the story of this person's life?

ZULEIKHA CHIKH

Leading the way to help women of all abilities and
cultures to enjoy the sport

Zuleikha Chikh loved everything about football – the training, the teamwork, the camaraderie. She had academic ambitions, having studied at University of Central Lancashire, obtaining an MSc in Sports Business Management. But she also had sporting dreams. As a woman of Indian and Algerian descent, she wanted to help more women like her share her love of football and all the positives that the game can bring.

And Zuleikha was not just a dreamer. She took action! Calling the local Football Development Officer, she was connected with a local club, where she became a coach and volunteer. Her football journey had begun.

One of her first goals was to get organised. So Zuleikha founded the University of Central Lancashire Women's Futsal Club. Futsal is a small-sided indoor version of football similar to the five-a-side game.

Keen to learn and meet new people, Zuleikha reached out to the community to find players. Soon, she had 17 women registered to play as

British Universities and Colleges Sport athletes, and 20 recreational players of 11 nationalities.

Her vision and dedication to making it a reality was paying off. Zuleikha was bringing football to more and more women from many different backgrounds. And the first competitive season was a hit on the pitch too, as her team came second in the league.

As chairperson of the Futsal club, Zuleikha is not only the chief organiser and fundraiser but also deals with the members' wants and needs.

Another of her leadership roles is on the Lancashire Football Association's Inclusion Advisory Group, where she offers advice on ensuring that football and futsal in the region are open to all.

Zuleikha enjoys seeing girls grow in confidence from the first time they kick a ball to eventually acquiring the skills to play competitive games.

In trying to increase the number of Asian women playing futsal, Zuleikha had to work out how to reach a community with a different culture from her own. These women were not necessarily sports-minded, so Zuleikha took a very personal approach.

Meeting with students from the university's Islamic Society, she took the trouble to explain not only what futsal is, but how the game can be enjoyed by women of all abilities and cultures.

The response was overwhelming. The women Zuleikha spent time with appreciated her efforts. And because of her knowledge and friendly approach, the number of Muslim-Asian girls taking part in futsal sessions has increased. More inclusion resulted in more diversity.

It was by no surprise that in 2019, Zuleikha was named in the Muslim Women in Sport Power List. The Power List showcases and provides a platform for the global community of Muslim Women in sport.

As part of a growing movement of women leading the way in sport, Zulheikha also feels that it just proves the increasing quality of influence from the female Muslim sports community and the role she plays in sport.

She thinks that to get what you want, you have to be willing to step out of your comfort zone and explore new opportunities. She says that young people should be encouraged to start their own projects and build a support network to help them achieve their goals. Zuleikha also believes that the most important thing of all is to be kind to yourself and others.

A LESSON TO SUPPORT GOOD MENTAL HEALTH: 'Look after yourself before you look after others. If you are not taking care of your sleep, hydration, exercise and diet you will get burnt out. If you feel like you are doing too much, slow down and be selective with what you are saying "yes" and "no" to.'

Questions to Think About:

1. Have you ever been discouraged from taking part in a sport or ever felt excluded? How did that make you feel? What did you do?

2. Zuleikha wants people to step out of their comfort zone. What does this mean and how could you do this?

3. What does inclusion mean and why is it important?

4. What does it mean to be kind to yourself? How can you be kind to yourself?

What are this person's signature strengths? How do you know? Provide evidence from the text.

How do you feel after reading the story of this person's life?

The Chronicles of Will Ryde & Awa Al- Jameel
Book 2
A KING'S ARMOUR
Rehan Khan

*'A fantastic feat of imagination. Incredibly engaging
and a rollicking read'*
Pete Kalu

*Following the daring recovery of the Staff of Moses, the elite Ruzgär unit embark on their second mission impossible. **Istanbul, 1592*** The arrival of a mysterious manuscript at the court of Sultan Murad III, claiming to know the location of the fabled Armour of King David, sends the Sultan into a frenzied desire to track it down.

Despite being the most powerful man in the world, he has never led his armies into battle and craves the protection of the legendary breastplate before he takes the field. It is to the elite Ruzgär unit that the Sultan turns once more to locate the Armour. This journey will be dangerous. Each warrior is aware that it could change their lives for ever, and that for some of them, this mission to find King David's Armour will be their last.

978-1-9164671-7-0

The Chronicles of Will Ryde & Awa Al- Jameel
Book 3
A DEMON'S TOUCH
Rehan Khan

'A fantastic fast-paced adventure, perfect reading'
***Children's Books Ireland* Recommended Reads**

Istanbul 1593. Will Ryde and Awa Al- Jameel are members of the Ruzgär Unit, an elite team of solders and specialists around the world that act on behalf of the supposedly mighty Ottoman Emperor, Sultan Murad III. The Ruzgär unit inadvertently released an ancient demon during the events of the previous book, *A King's Armour*. The demon now lurks within the bowels of the city coinciding with Sultan Murad III bringing friend and foe to Istanbul, to convene the world's grandest trade fair.

Returning from their previous mission with the death of their Commander weighing heavily upon them, there is no respite for the Ruzgär unit, as they are declared traitors to the Ottoman Empire and banished from the legendary Janissary order. Even the recovery of the fabled Armour of David, so prized by the Sultan, is not enough to prevent this.

Now, desperate and on the run, Will must turn to the sinister Earl of Rothminster as an unlikely protector. Meanwhile Awa and the remaining Ruzgär, outcasts as far as the authorities are concerned, are called upon by their small band of supporters to protect the very people who have declared them enemies of the empire. All roads lead to Istanbul and all who traverse it, will be plagued by a demon's touch.

978-1-913109-81-3

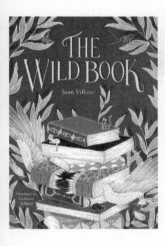

THE WILD BOOK
Juan Villoro
Translated from the Spanish by Lawrence Schimel

'A must read for book-lovers everywhere'
Book Trust

'A beautifully written ode to the inherent magic of books'
Foreword Reviews

Thirteen-year-old Juan's summer is off to a terrible start. First, his parents separate. Then, almost as bad, Juan is sent away to his strange Uncle Tito's house for the entire holiday! Who wants to live with an oddball recluse who has zigzag eyebrows, drinks fifteen cups of smoky tea a day, and lives inside a huge, mysterious library?

As Juan adjusts to his new life among dusty shelves, he notices something odd: the books move on their own! He rushes to tell Uncle Tito, who lets his nephew in on a secret: Juan is a Princeps Reader, which means books respond magically to him, and he's the only one who can find the elusive, never-before-read *Wild Book*. But will Juan and his new friend Catalina get to *The Wild Book* before the wicked, story-stealing *Pirate Book* does?

978-1-9164671-0-1

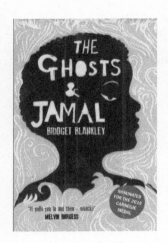

THE GHOSTS & JAMAL
Bridget Blankley

Nominated for the 2019 Carnegie Medal

'It pulls you in and then – whack'
Melvin Burgess

Set somewhere in Africa, *The Ghosts & Jamal* is an intriguing story, touching on religion, terrorism and internal conflicts, following a young orphan who is negotiating an unforgiving society. Waking up in the aftermath of a terrorist attack, 13-year-old Jamal tries to piece together what has happened whilst simultaneously trying to evade capture by the attackers. It soon becomes clear that he has been living in a separate outhouse from his family on account of the "bad spirits" that plague him.

As he wanders around his family's compound, he comes across red canisters leaking yellow gas, which he works out were the weapon that killed his family, and he begins calling the gas "ghosts". With his family dead, he begins to search for his grandfather who he hardly knows; when his grandfather turns him away he keeps walking. On his journey he passes out and is picked up by a patrolling soldier. He is taken to a hospital where he is treated for the "spirits", or rather, his epilepsy. Jamal escapes and on doing so, he wanders bewildered around the city. On the way he meets prejudice, exploitation and friendship, before finally discovering that it is people, not ghosts, that have killed his family, and they have plans to keep on killing.

978-1-908446-63-3

WHITE HORSE
Yan Ge
Translated from the Chinese by Nicky Harman

2020 Warwick Prize for Women in Translation

'A talented writer'
The Irish Times

'With the most amazing Chinese brush art
throughout. Superb stuff from Yan Ge'
New China Daily

Yun Yun lives in a small West China town with her widowed father and an uncle, aunt and older cousin who live nearby. One day, her once-secure world begins to fall apart. Through her eyes, we observe her cousin, Zhang Qing, keen to dive into the excitements of adolescence but clashing with repressive parents. Ensuing tensions reveal that the relationship between the two families are founded on a terrible lie.

978-1-908446-98-5

THE STRIKER SERIES
YOU'RE NOT PROPER
Book1
Tariq Mehmood

'I love it, a cracking good book!'
Lemn Sissay

'Contemporary and hard-hitting! High on impact and highly engaging'
Jake Hope

With her dad a Pakistani and her mother white Christian, Karen thinks she's not proper white and doesn't quite fit in... anywhere. So she's made a choice: she's switching sides.

She's going to convert to Islam to try to find her true identity.

But Shamshad, her Hijab wearing school mate, isn't making things easy for her. Is Shamshad really any more proper than her? Trouble and turmoil await in the old textile mill town in Northern England, as school battles are replaced by family troubles, name-calling turns into physical fights and secrets are unveiled.

978-1-908446-68-8

THE STRIKER SERIES
THE SILENT STRIKER
Book 2
Pete Kalu

*'Full to the brim with the joy, heartache and passion of
the beautiful game'*
Melvin Burgess

*'A story that takes you through every emotion a young
school boy goes through'*
Dotun Adebayo, BBC Radio 5

Marcus is the best player in his football team. He's so good that there's a very real chance he'll be signed by Manchester United. But when he discovers he may be losing his hearing, his whole world falls to pieces and he finds himself having to put them back together on his own. But is this feeling of isolation real or just a consequence of his own behaviour? While dealing with parents, friends and first girlfriends, Marcus gradually understands that accepting the help of others is ultimately an acceptance of self.

A novel about friendship and family, *The Silent Striker* explores the issue of disability, and deafness, and the different ways in which we can choose to handle it.

978-1-908446-69-5

THE STRIKER SERIES
BEING ME
Book 3
Pete Kalu

'*A witty, lively novel of growing up female, black and middle-class in contemporary London*'
Carol Leeming, Author

There's never a dull day with Adele: she's a star footballer with a rotten family, an aching heart, and an impossible *frenemy*. As pressures at school and home mount, will she overcome all or will she crash and burn?

Fighting with her best friend Michaela, texting and kissing her first boyfriend and dealing with her screwed up family, you would think this girl was busy enough, yet she still finds the time to get herself into trouble. When everything collapses, Adele realizes she can only rely on herself to sort things out.

Adele could be any teenage girl living in Britain in this day and age: strong, humanly flawed and extremely charismatic. *Being Me* is the perfect companion to *The Silent Striker*, a feminine take on the football world, being a teenager and figuring out who you are.

978-1-908446-70-1

THE STRIKER SERIES
ZOMBIE XI
Book 4
Pete Kalu

'*A feast of fun and imagination*'
Courttia Newland

Leonard sits on the substitutes' bench, and never asked to play . . . and it's not as if the Ducie High football team is any good: they get beaten, time after time. Then everything changes. After a game near a nuclear power plant, a weird energy passes through Leonard, and that night in bed he is visited by zombies . . .

The ghostly players from the winning 1966 England World Cup team tell him that if he follows their instructions, not only will he get off the bench – but Ducie High XI will start to take control. Leonard obeys, and the team's prospects surge. But what is the price of the zombies' involvement? How high will that price be – and what pound of *living* flesh will they demand?

ZOMBIES XI is a story about football, friendship, family and cross-cultural teen relationships. Its humour, drama - and occasional shivers - send this book straight to the back of the net

978-1-908446-71-8